DECEIT

Cover Design by MadHat Books

Editor Josie Cruz

Connect with Rebecca Clark

DECEIT

Library of Congress Control Number:

ISBN-10:0-692-72772-8

ISBN-13:978-0-692-72772-0

This book is for Alexis

"Do not follow where the path may lead. Go instead where there is no path and leave a trail."

Ralph Waldo Emerson

Table of Contents

Chapter Seventeen

Chapter Eighteen

Chapter Nineteen

Prologue

IT MELTED HIS HEART STARING down at his little girl tucked into bed. Who would have thought the galaxy's militia leader would have a soft spot? In the nearly three years since the birth of his daughter, he had walked a fine line between keeping her safe and exposing the truth.

This moment had been coming for some time. However, he hadn't realized just how hard it would be to let go. He wanted to hold onto her forever, but he knew he couldn't. Keeping her safe was more important than keeping her.

He leaned down and kissed her forehead, inhaling the scent of her baby shampoo as the blonde flyaway hairs tickled his nose. That familiar smell made his heart swell. How do you go from being truly happy to alone? He wondered how he was supposed to walk away from his everything.

Before he left the room, he switched on her favorite moon and star night-light. Turning around, he saw her big green eyes staring back at him. It broke his heart to think this was the last time he would be tucking her into bed. He wished with everything he was that he could freeze this moment in time. He wished he could wake up and spend just one more day with her. But he knew he couldn't.

"Goodnight, Daddy. I love you." She flipped onto her side and cuddled her stuffed bunny under her nose. The covers came up to her shoulders, and all he could see was her fine, blonde hair.

"I love you, too, baby girl." He always replied the same way, and he wouldn't change that tonight. He didn't want her to think anything was different. Selfishly, he wanted to remember her just this way—safe and happy.

He watched her from the doorway as her breathing settled into a rhythmic pattern, then exited her room and pulled the door shut behind him. There was no other option. He had to leave her. Being around her created an unsafe environment. Deep down, he knew this would be harder for him; soon, she would forget him, but he would always be thinking of her, forever.

The realization hit him that if he saw his daughter again, she would be much older and the damage would be done. She would know that he'd left her and she might never forgive him. However, that was the chance he had to take. No matter what he chose, there would be enough regret to last a lifetime.

Often, he wondered what would have happened if he hadn't taken his daughter away, if he'd told his wife the truth. Would she have changed her evil ways? He kept replaying the last day he spent with his wife over and over again in his head. They were the power couple, Kalus and Queen Alala. He couldn't help imagining the fairytale that could have been. But there was more to it than that, and he had to focus on the facts. Relying on emotions or contemplating what could have been was useless.

He had to face his future, a future without his daughter.

"Please take care of her. My daughter is everything to me. Protect her with everything you are." His voice cracked.

"You know I will, Kalus," she replied.

"I trust you. That's why you're here. I know you'll love her as I do." He tried to smile, but he couldn't overcome the despair that washed through him.

"I'll do everything in my power to protect her," she said gently, trying to comfort him with her words. "She will feel love because I love her like I would my own child."

That fateful night when she'd helped him stage his own daughter's death now wove the three of them together. Indeed, once it was safe, they'd fled together, leaving a trail of lies to cover their tracks.

He took a few steps back and glanced over at his daughter's bedroom door, then solemnly strode toward the front door, all while the pain of losing his daughter bore a hole right through his gut, leaving him breathless. The only thing that kept him moving was the well-being of his daughter. If they found him, they would find her. He knew that would be worse than leaving her here to live her life.

Here, she had a chance to be happy, even if it wasn't forever. If they found her now, he knew she would only become a bargaining chip, and go to the highest bidder.

"If an emergency arises, you know how to reach me. When and if that happens, there will be no going back," he warned. "The life you live here will be over."

She nodded curtly to show her understanding.

He opened his arms and enveloped her. Even though she was slight, he knew she could protect his daughter. Her training had been thorough and systematic, giving her the tools to protect herself and now his daughter. "Goodbye," he whispered, "and thank you for all that you have done, and for all that you have left behind." He kissed the top of her head and slowly crept away from her bed. He didn't wait for a response. He left and didn't look back.

She watched from the window as he disappeared into the darkness. She knew the task that lay in front of her would be anything but easy. She also knew she would die before she let anything happen to that innocent little girl.

One

"Don't go!" I holler at the figure dissolving next to me.

He bats his long lashes and the corners of his lips move upward in a sly grin. "I'll see you again."

I watch his lips move, wanting more. "When?"

I can't help but want answers. These recurring dreams of him have to mean something, right? Those mysterious blue eyes haunt my waking hours.

"Tonight." With that one word, he spins around and marches away from me. Fog swirls around his feet, then envelops his body, leaving me standing alone in a field of flowers, waiting to be plucked back into reality.

Bewildered by the sight of my legs fading, I know it's only a matter of moments before the rest of my body follows. My surroundings begin to waft away. The dull buzzing grows with each passing second. I'm now peering down at myself from above and witnessing my journey back into reality.

The constant beep, beep, beep chips away at my consciousness. I fight the urge to open my eyes. I know what awaits me. I want to spend a few more minutes remembering his gorgeous face.

Reluctantly, I peel my sweaty body off the bedsheet and cross the room to put my alarm clock out of its misery. If my alarm were bedside, I would never make it to school on time.

I venture back into my dream while I shower. Most mornings I feel robbed of a restful sleep, but today in particular, I really enjoyed seeing him.

I rinse my hair and speedily shave my legs. I complete the same routine every day, even though I always wear the same boring outfits, which usually consist of jeans. I grab my towel and quickly dry myself.

"Today is going to be miserable. I hate Mondays," I mumble while tossing around my clothes looking for the most comfortable t-shirt I own. Big, ominous, black clouds roll by my bedroom window as if confirming my glum prediction. Thunder erupts in the distance, sending chills down my spine. I'll have to run to school if I want to make it before my hair, so carefully straight-ironed, frizzes up. Envisioning the stares that I'll get, I speed up my preparations.

When I step in front of the mirror, my jaw drops. What happened to my eyes? The whites are laden with red, clashing with the green irises. My lids are puffy, and the normally pale skin beneath my eyes appears bruised. "Why are my eyes this scary? I just woke up." Half expecting an answer from the image in the mirror, I sigh and keep moving. I don't want to get stuck in the rain.

New England weather is something of a mystery. Spring is just as fickle as fall. One day you could be basking in the sun, sipping lemonade, and just days later, winter can rear its ugly head with a few inches of snow, rain, or sleet. At least the weather might add some pizzazz to my life, which is so lacking in excitement it's embarrassing—a teenager's worst nightmare.

Currently, I live vicariously through my best friend, who resides in an entirely different state. Her stories of New York City are never boring or mundane. I wait eagerly to hear her reports of dating calamities and weekly updates every Sunday.

I've lived in a suburb of Boston, Massachusetts, for my whole life—almost seventeen years—and I've always had the notion that I don't belong here. It seems as if I've been stranded in a city with people who don't speak my language. Some mornings, I find myself staring at my reflection in the bathroom mirror, a shell of what should be, waiting for something, anything. I need a telltale sign or signal that I'm, indeed, living the wrong life.

My life is all about routine. The hot boy in my dreams night after night is the only truly exciting event happening. They take place somewhere with vast magenta skylines, purple-stemmed flowers with green velvet petals, a trio of orange moons, and the most recent addition—a boy who would make a Greek god jealous.

I can't be sure if he is a real Greek god, but he has the body: mesmerizing, aquamarine eyes, dark-brown hair framing a stoic face punctuated with a chiseled chin, broad shoulders and bulging muscles that can hardly be contained by his t-shirt—it's all enough to make any god envious and every girl swoon. He isn't frightening or scary. In fact, he is quite the opposite. He knows my name, and he addresses me as if we're old friends. I'm sure it's just another dream that teases me with the exciting life I want, I tell myself as I try but fail to get his image out of my head.

Last night, he reached out to me, and it seemed different. I can't describe why this is a big deal, why this dream felt so real—I know it's just a dream.

"Alexa, you're going to be late!" Mom shouts. Why does she always find it necessary to scream up the steps as I'm about to dart down them?

Entering the kitchen, the smell of coffee swirls around me, instantly energizing me. "Mom, when have I ever been late?" I ask, exasperated.

She winks and shrugs, making her chin-length, dark-brown hair swish back and forth. She hides her smirk behind the newspaper. In true mom fashion, she quickly changes the subject. "I might be late tonight. I'm covering someone's day shift. If I'm later than seven thirty, I'll call you. But there's leftover pizza in the fridge and plenty of food in the freezer."

"Mom, I'm going to be seventeen years old. I'm sure I can find something for dinner," I reply peevishly. "I always do, don't I?" My mom is never home for dinner, but I'm certainly old enough to take care of myself. I don't begrudge my mother's career as a nurse working the night shift. She's provided a great life for the two of us.

"I know...I can still worry about you, though, can't I?"

I roll my eyes and kiss her cheek. "Sure, Mom. You will anyway, no matter what I say."

"Have a good day, sweetie. I will see you tonight." She winks one of her big blue eyes at me again.

"Bye, Mom." I grab my book bag and fly out the door.

The storm is close now. I quickly pull my pink hoodie up over my hair, resenting the need to hurry to school. Mondays are the worst days of the week. They always seem longer than usual, and the gossip about the weekend constantly reminds me that my life is boring.

"Alexa, can you please give us the answer to number two?" Great, Mr. Riley caught me daydreaming again in his class.

I watch him pace back and forth in front of the room, expecting my answer, which I don't have. I can detect the other students' eyes all swinging toward me, their stares penetrating holes right through me. My ears burn and heat trails up my neck into my face. I know at that point, my normally pale skin now gleams watermelon red.

I can't help it; all I can think about is him—the boy from my dreams. Exotic blue eyes, and the way he sings my name...captivating. His broad shoulders and athletic body are permanently singed into my brain. I really can't stop thinking about him. If only the dream were true and he was real! The students around here would treat me differently if I showed up with *him* on my arm as my boyfriend. I almost laugh out loud at that ridiculous notion.

Mandy, the girl in front of me, swivels her head around to see what's taking me so long to answer. Her red banana curls bounce up and down and, for a moment, I'm transfixed by the perfection of each ringlet. How does she get her hair so Marie-Claire perfect? No wonder she's the captain of the cheerleading team. My mop would never look like that. I have straight, blonde hair that doesn't do much of anything except frizz. I straighten it daily, hoping to enforce the no-frizz law. I keep it shoulder length—anything longer takes forever to straighten.

I stare at Mandy. She scrunches her freckled nose at me and mouths something. I'm not sure what she is trying to say. I glance back up at the teacher; he has halted his pacing to stare at me, as well. Sweat trickles down my temples and I wish I could shrink into my seat and disappear. I've absolutely no idea what he's asking me, but if I request that he repeat the question, everyone will know I wasn't paying attention.

Just as I clear my throat, ready to give a random answer, a voice speaks up behind me. "I believe the answer is prokaryotic cell."

Mr. Riley looks right through me to the source of the answer. "Yes, Michael, you're correct." He launches himself right back into his pacing, one of his signature moves. Students frequently link this pacing to his overt craziness.

I can feel the students' eyes shifting from me to the front of the class. I take a deep breath and try to follow along. The class isn't all that bad. I enjoy science, and biology itself is very interesting. I like learning about cells and how things work. It doesn't bother me that most people refer to me as a nerd or a geek. I'm just having a hard time concentrating on anything but these dreams.

Mr. Riley stops at the board and writes *Test on Friday*. He stands there scratching his head as if he's planning to add more, but he doesn't. Mr. Riley is an odd guy. Some girls swoon over his handsome, disguised-as-nerdy looks, his light-brown hair casually perfect, his green eyes framed with his unique tortoiseshell glasses. Some of the boys copy his eyewear in hopes of attracting girls. He always insists on writing on the old chalkboard, even though there are new whiteboards installed in every classroom. He's also always covered in chalk, because he constantly leans up against the board or writes on it, then touches his pants or puts his hands in his pockets. It's like he's creating his very own artwork.

"Don't forget to study for the exam," Mr. Riley announces before the bell rings.

The bell interrupts my mental examination of Mr. Riley. Quickly, I turn around to thank Michael for saving me with the answer. "Hey, Michael, thanks—I was totally daydreaming before. I never would have answered that question correctly." Michael lives a few blocks away from me. He was the new kid last year; of course, unlike me, he immediately fit right in.

Michael smiles and nods. He has perfect, movie-star-white teeth and a face that melts hearts. Instantly, my own face flushes. Did I over-share by admitting to daydreaming? Also, I hadn't realized just how attractive Michael is until this moment.

"No problem, Alexa, but you could make it up to me," he replies. "You can tutor me for the biology exam. I was in

your math class last year, so I know how smart you are."
Eyebrows raised, Michael awaits my response.

Michael is thin, but tall. He has the best hair, longer
on the top and always styled toward the front. The girls
refer to Michael's hair as the best "Beiber-do" in the school.
Other boys at school have a similar hairstyle, but his shade
of brown is a unique hazelnut color.

"Possibly. When would you want to study? The test
is Friday and it's only Monday." I divert my eyes to my bag
and pretend to search for something important.

"How about we study after school today?" Michael
opens his eyes wide, waiting for my response, which
definitely surprises me.

"Okay. Why don't you come by around four o'clock
this afternoon?" Can this really be happening? No one ever
gives me the time of day at school, especially an attractive
boy with the coveted Beiber-do.

"That sounds great," he responds. "Oh, yeah, I almost
forgot to ask... Are you going to the dance on Saturday?"

The idea of pinching myself came to mind. Did he
really just ask me about the homecoming dance? "We will
do well on the exam," I counter with a nod and a reassuring
smile. He continues to stare at me, as if he's waiting for me
to say something.

"And the dance?" he asks.

"Um, I'm not sure about the dance." I swallow.
"Maybe. I haven't decided yet." Why is he asking me this?
Maybe this is a joke. However, gazing into those big, brown
eyes isn't torturous. Michael and I've always been cordial,
and I even had multiple conversations with him last year.
But this is different, more personal.

"But isn't it your birthday?" he asks playfully.

I must be dreaming—how does he even know it's
my birthday? And why does he care? I watch him run his
hands through his thick, lustrous hair and realize it's very
similar in color to his eyes.

"Come on, Alexa, it's like the homecoming dance is scheduled on that day to celebrate your birthday. Okay, that's cheesy—forget I said that."

We both laugh.

"It's my birthday, but my best friend is coming to visit, and we're planning to go out to dinner. Maybe we'll stop by the dance afterward." I say this knowing there's no way I'm going to talk Sheri into going to a dance. Sheri has been my friend for years, and she's never been one to conform to high school life.

We grew up next door to each other until her father's job moved their family to the Big Apple. It has been a hard four years without her, but at least we keep in touch weekly. The only good thing is that Sheri's father promised her a car on her sixteenth birthday, and he kept his promise. Sheri uses her car to visit once a month. I'm really looking forward to seeing her this weekend. I can't wait to tell someone about my crazy dreams and to be reassured that I'm not losing my mind.

"So, maybe I'll see you there, Michael," I continue. "Anyways, I need to run to gym class. Coach hates it when we're late."

He brushes my arm as he moves out of my way so I can get past him. I wonder if he meant to do that. I've never gotten that close to him before. The scent of Dial soap and an earthy cologne tickle my nose.

"Okay, you better get to the gym. I'll catch up with you later." He flashes a toothy grin and I run for the door.

Why did Michael ask if I was going to the dance? How did he remember my birthday?

The sound of my cell phone vibrating in my bag startles me.

A text from Sheri: *OMG so sorry I have a family obligation Saturday night.*

I text her back: *No problem. BTW I need to talk to you!*

I wait for a response, but nothing. I really want to tell her about the handsome man that visited me in my sleep most nights. I need to be reassured that I'm not losing my mind.

Lately, it's weird between us ever since she got a serious boyfriend. Damon's presence always trumps our monthly visits. Last time she drove here, she left early so she could spend more time with him. I think it's ridiculous since she sees him daily at school.

Great, another lonely birthday while Mom works the night shift. Oh, well. Maybe she can take it off. She rarely takes any time off from work, though. She's always complaining that they're understaffed, and if she took off a night, she'd be afraid that patients would go untreated or ignored. Mom can be a little dramatic.

At least I only have one more class, and then home to study. I woke up knowing today was going to be miserable, but instead, it's just plain peculiar.

Two

SURPRISINGLY ENOUGH, THE STUDYING with Michael is going very well. It's so easy to talk to him. He does know a lot about biology, so I'm sure he will do well on the test.

After studying for a few hours, Michael starts in on the whole dance thing again. He continues to pester me with questions like, "Why wouldn't you want to go?" or, "It's so much fun. Have you ever been to a school dance?"

The more he talks about the dance, the more I entertain the idea of actually going. He seems so genuinely excited, it's becoming contagious. Homecoming is a big night in a typical teenager's high school life. Why shouldn't I go and enjoy it like most people my age? Just because I feel like an outsider doesn't mean I have to act like one. This is something I would never do alone, but with someone—especially a boy—it could be fun.

"Fine, I'll go," I finally say. "You talked me into it. Also, I need to see the gym for myself. I don't believe it's possible to transform our old gym into a believable venue for a dance."

We both smile at my admission.

Contentment fills me. Who would have thought committing to a high school experience would leave me so happy? Why had I never partaken before? It's time I livened up my not-so-exciting life.

"I promise, you will not be disappointed," he quickly says. "The gym always looks magical on dance nights, especially with it being homecoming. What about your friend from out of town? Will she be coming, too?"

"Actually, she can't make it. She had a family thing pop up." Even as I'm saying it, I don't believe it. She probably wants to be with Damon. But even though Sheri can't make it, the evening has the potential to be a fun, memorable birthday. Hopefully, Sheri will come visit soon so we can catch up. I've a feeling I'll have a lot to tell her. I still can't believe she hasn't answered my text message from earlier today.

I also can't believe that the more time Michael and I spend together studying, the more at ease I'm with him. It's nice to get to know someone. Maybe I can get the hang of being social. I usually keep to myself at school because I've this weird belief that I'm constantly being judged. The kids in my grade are snobby and more wrapped up in what they have or want. I've never had the privilege to be extravagant, nor would I want to be. I'm just wired differently. I was also raised in a single-income household. I don't have parents with trust funds and high-paying careers.

The only quirky thing I notice while studying with Michael is that he's constantly staring at me. It's so obvious that when I glance down at my book, I sense his eyes on me. "Why are you always staring at me? Shouldn't you be reviewing the text as well?" I try, asking playfully, then instantly regret bringing it up.

"Um, I'm not always staring at you," he replies hesitantly. "It's just, sometimes I think you remind me of someone I know from where I used to live. I didn't mean anything by it. Plus, you're easy to gaze at," he adds with a smirk that makes me instantly blush.

For some reason, we get along so well. It's a feeling of comfort that only comes from knowing someone a long time. As for that last comment he made, I think he was just flirting; I'm not one hundred percent sure, but that's what it sounded like.

"Alexa, what color dress do you think you'll wear to the dance?"

His question catches me completely off guard. Why would he care? "I'm not sure. Why do you want to know?" I plant my eyes in the book. I don't want him to see the confusion that's probably showing on my face.

"Well, if we go together, I want to wear the same colors so we match—if that's okay with you?"

Now Michael appears a little uncomfortable, so I quickly nod and smile. "Okay, sounds good." A warm and fuzzy thrill spreads through me. I wonder if this is a normal experience for Mandy and her circle of friends.

Just as we're wrapping up the session, my mother calls up from the stairs, saying it's time for Michael to go home. I didn't even hear her come home from work. I'm just glad that she received my text message that he would be here and not to embarrass me. I glance at the clock and I can't believe it's after nine o'clock. The time flew by.

I stand up, sensing his eyes following my every move. I open the door to my bedroom and he jumps up, wraps his arm around my waist, and guides me out of the room. The touch of his arm sends an exhilarating ripple through my body. I walk slowly to the stairs, hoping he won't drop his hand prematurely.

We bounce down the stairs laughing at some corny joke Michael recites. Even though I don't think it's funny, I laugh anyway. Which is what Sheri would probably call flirting.

At the bottom of the stairs, Michael turns around and peers directly into my eyes. "Alexa, thanks for helping me. Now I've absolutely no reason to do horrible on another biology exam. I'll see you tomorrow. Do you want me to walk by and pick you up for school in the morning?" Still wearing the grin his joke has conjured, he waits for my answer.

"Yeah, that sounds great." I don't want to seem too eager, but I'm. It's sometimes so lonesome walking to school everyday by myself. "Good night, Michael."

After I shut the door, I whirl around on my heels and just stand there a moment. Is this really happening? Could he actually like me?

My mother's voice interrupts the firing squad of questions blasting inside my head. "Alexa, honey, how was studying with Michael?"

"It was good. I think we will both do well on the test on Friday. I'm going to bed now. Good night, Mom."

"Night, honey, see you in the morning."

I scale the stairs two at a time in a sudden burst of newfound energy. I can't help smiling and thinking about how easy it is to talk to him, a boy. Maybe high school this year won't be so horrible.

I catch a glimpse of myself in the mirror. It has been a long time since I've seen a genuine smile on my face. I don't recognize myself but I like it. Tonight is going to be a challenging night to fall asleep. All I can do is think about his touch and how comfortable I am with him.

The smell of lilacs permeates my senses and makes it hard to focus. Once again, I'm sitting in a field of purple-stemmed, green flowers. The fresh lilac smell is so strong, I bring my hand up to cover my nose and mouth. I reach down with my other hand to touch the green petals. One by one, they fall off and float up toward the sky. I can't keep myself from touching another; they're velvety soft, unlike any type of flower I've ever encountered. I watch the loose petal sail high above me toward the cotton-candy-colored sky while the whispering wind tickles my ears.

Usually in these dreams, I'm watching myself from above. This time, I'm fully experiencing it. My senses are overloaded with the smells, textures, and noises.

I slowly rise to explore, one step at a time, my bare feet sinking into the ground beneath me as I venture toward the tree line. Thinking I'm walking over quicksand, I panic and hasten my pace, eyes on the honeydew-green leaves on the trees looming before me as they sway in a fresh breeze. As I distance myself from the flowers, I'm finally able to remove my hand from my mouth and take a deep breath.

My feet continue to sink into the cool ground as I trek deeper into the woods. The magenta sky swirls over my head and a thunderous roar rings in my ears. Daylight is transforming into dusk. I find the darkness unnerving and change direction, heading back toward the field. The orderly columns of tree trunks thin, and I emerge back into the field. The three moons overhead begin to flicker with an intense yellow hue.

My heart pounds and exhaustion spreads throughout my body. I get this prickly awareness that someone is watching me, which only makes my heart pound faster. Too nervous to validate this dreadful alertness by searching for the source, I continue forward. How am I going to get home? Where am I?

Now that I'm out of the forest and far enough away from its disconcerting darkness, I collapse to my knees. Goosebumps blossom over my skin and an eerie sensation gnaws at my gut.

"You shouldn't be here." The authoritative, masculine voice splinters the silence in my ears. I whirl to see who is there. But I see nothing.

Frantic, I jump up and draw a deep breath before turning a slow circle, seeking who might have spoken to me. I'm the only one standing there.

The darkness is disseminating over the field from the forest as if creeping toward me. I scramble forward, trying to stay ahead of the impending gloom, but my fatigue is growing and my momentum slows. I glance up to see that the three moons are no longer yellow; they now resemble giant, red fireballs that are snowballing toward the field.

I need to run.

I use every last bit of effort to flee. It doesn't last long. My muscles throb and my legs slow. I physically cannot move anymore—my legs are useless and my lungs burn. I collapse on the field and bury my head in my arms, waiting for either the darkness to engulf me, or the fireballs to crash into me.

"One, two, three, four..." I murmur to myself.

Ever since I was young, I've counted to calm myself down. It works; my chest rises and sinks more evenly as I brace myself for impact.

"Alexa, you need to go home and wake up." The familiar voice in my head sounds like that of the gorgeous boy with the blue eyes.

"Alexa, wake up!"

My mom's voice pulls me back into reality, but my eyelids are heavy; prying them open is like heaving concrete pallets. Once they're up, they lighten, and I blink a few times and find myself back in my bedroom. The framed photos of Sheri and I sitting on my dresser replace the field of purple-stemmed, green flowers. Exhausted, I raise my head from my pillow, which is a major feat...

"Alexa, it's almost six o'clock!" I open my eyes again to see the light sifting through the blinds on my window. I can sense my cat Fluffy nearby, probably staring at me. Most mornings when I wake, she's close by, peering at me as if she, too, is experiencing my dreamland. That would explain her skittish behavior lately. I sit up and turn around to see her perched on the edge of my pillow, staring at me intently, as if she knows what I just endured.

The smell of strawberry frosted Pop Tarts seeps under my bedroom door. That's the telltale sign that I'm running late.

"Mom, I'm up! Jumping in the shower right now," I yell down to her so she doesn't come up and give me a speech about why school is important and how high school is only a few years blah, blah—every day is a new blah, blah.

I often wonder why school has to start so early. There have been studies completed on how teenagers should get eight and a half to nine hours of sleep daily. And that's impossible when you add up all of the homework we get. I'm lucky if I get seven hours. To top it off, lately my dreams make sleep more work than rest. At least I won't be distracted all day with thoughts of the blue-eyed boy from my dreams, since last night he was, sadly, a no-show.

I need to find something to wear that will impress Michael, but what's staring back at me is a closet full of t-shirts in every color, a stack of jeans, and my go-to boots. I really want to wear something other than my usual. Moving the clothes around, I find a green tunic with the tags still on it. I slip it over my wet hair and wiggle myself into a pair of black, never worn, leggings.

"Perfect; this will be adorable with my black flats." I can't help but smile at my new outfit and the new me. I reach behind my head and tear off the tags, "I'm definitely keeping this."

Quickly, I dart into the bathroom to style my hair. I can't be late because Michael is walking with me to school. I wonder if he is as excited to see me as I'm to see him. I'm sure I'm reading way too much into our studying encounter, but I can't wait to see him. A fleeting thought makes me nervous... What if he forgets to pick me up and runs right past me?

I shake it off, pull myself together, and continue trying to control the few frizzy, flyaway blonde strands still tickling my face. My green eyes stare back at me in the mirror with a glow of anticipation. The green from the tunic makes my eye color pop. Maybe Michael will notice? I roll my eyes at my own silly thought. Why would he notice?

Just as I finish applying my pink lip gloss, the doorbell rings. I fly down the stairs, stop at the bottom, and take a deep breath. I open the door. He is standing on the front step, wearing a welcoming smile. A surge of excitement washes over me the way it did when I stood in line to ride a roller coaster for the very first time. When he steps through the doorway, his height reminds me that I'm wearing flats instead of my usual military-style boots.

"Wow, your eyes, Alexa. They're absolutely stunning."

The heartfelt comment makes me blush. I guess he did notice. I smile in return and gather my belongings, quickly turning the subject from me with, "Thanks. How did you sleep last night?"

"I slept well. I'm a little nervous about the exam Friday. I always assume I'm going to do better than I actually do. I go in thinking it's in the bag, then a few days later, I get my test back and I got a C, or even worse, a D." His smile disappears and a more serious Michael is staring at me.

I can tell this is really bothering him, and I sympathize even though I've no idea what it's like to get a C or a D. Usually, it doesn't matter if I study or not, because I always pass with an A. That's why I'm number three in the class of seven hundred and twenty students. Part of me wishes I found the work more difficult so I could relate.

Maybe then, other students would see me as normal. The only thing really difficult in high school, for me, is the social part.

The weird thing about school and tests is that I only have to see the material once to do well on a test. I have a great memory; my mom refers to it as my photographic memory, and she assures me that my father was the same way.

"I think you'll do great. Plus, you still have a few more days to review the material." I give him a quick nod and my best hopeful smile to confirm my intentions. I can't help noticing how his blue sweatshirt pulls out the lighter hues in his brown eyes, making them appear a totally different color. He's so hot.

"Alexa, don't forget your breakfast." My mother walks into the living room carrying my Pop Tart in a to-go napkin. How embarrassing. Now he'll know my mom still makes my breakfast for me. If I could melt into the floorboards beneath me, I would.

"Thanks, Mom," I mumble as she winks and hands me my still-warm Pop Tart. The scent of strawberry wafts up to taunt me, but I don't dare eat in front of Michael. I place it in my bag and hope he won't think this is too weird. I uncomfortably shrug, not knowing what to say. He smiles and opens the door for me. Just like that, we're on our way to school.

The walk goes far too quickly, with us both talking nonstop. It's truly odd how much we have in common. He makes being me so easy. I wonder why we didn't talk much last year in tenth grade. Most likely because he was the new kid, and everyone loves the new kid. He was always hanging with Mandy's crowd, even though he wasn't a jock. His "new" status held enough pull to get him into any clique he desired. This city has so few new people moving in, the popular kids cling to them like little bloodsuckers.

When we arrive at school, all the cool people are hanging out in the parking lot next to their expensive rides that mommy and daddy bought them. At least I'm not walking by them alone. Even though I'm in flats, I know I appear taller. I confidently stride by them showing a less self-conscious version of myself.

"Hey, Michael," Mandy calls out as we walk past her group.

"Hi, Mandy," Michael replies.

Today just might be a good day, I think as we enter the school. Michael grins and leans in to whisper in my ear, "I'm going to run to my locker before class, so I'll catch up with you later, Alexa."

His breath tickles my ear and a flash of heat consumes me. All I can do is stand there in the hallway for a few moments, certain that I might pass out if I move too soon. He was mere inches from my face, in public. "Um...oh, okay...sounds good. Have fun in class," I manage.

He gives me a quick, charming smile and he's gone.

The idea of going to class isn't so bad. Now I've something to occupy my time. I shuffle to Spanish class and plop down in my seat with a grin on my face.

After that exhilaration wears off, though, classes are the usual—boring. How can anything beat my morning walk to school with Michael? The great thing is, I spend less time obsessing about my weird dreams when I can focus on trying to catch a glimpse of Michael in between classes. I never noticed before whom he hung out with.

Unfortunately, the only times I see him today are at lunch, when he's only there for a minute, and when he walks me to English class. The highlight is biology class; even though he sits behind me and I can't see him, I can sense his presence.

As soon as the final bell rings, elation fills me and I'm hopeful that I'll see Michael on the way home and we can walk together. I go to my locker and pretend to get something, even though I barely ever stop there after school. But I know I have a good view of Michael's locker from mine.

Just as I'm about to give up, a hand grazes my back. I know from the warm, tingling touch it's Michael. I turn to face him, trying to hide my relief that he found me.

"How was your day?" He smiles while taking the Spanish book from my hands. "I'll carry this."

"Thanks." I hope my shock isn't too obvious. No one has ever carried my books before. I thought that kind of thing only happened in movies. "My day was good. Spanish was a little more boring than normal, but I survived. How was your day?"

"The usual, nothing worth mentioning. But it seems to be getting better now." He let out a loud sigh. "I can't believe you're in advanced placement Spanish with Señor Paulino. I have him for regular Spanish Two, and I'm drowning in all the work."

I can tell by Michael's voice that he's again being hard on himself. "Well, I can always help you. I've been taking Spanish since sixth grade."

He reaches out and brushes a strand of hair from my face. My stomach instantly flips. He smiles and responds, "Thanks, Alexa. I know I can always count on you."

We leave the school and walk home slowly, enjoying the late fall day. We talk about everything that happened at school. I can easily get used to this. He's not only smart but also nice, and so adorable. Things are turning around for me.

Alexa Jenkinson may have a great junior year after all.

I have to call Sheri and tell her about this, I think with a secret thrill.

Three

"ALEXA, HOW LONG HAVE YOU BEEN HERE?"

How does he know my name? Well, it's my fantasy state, so he can know my name if I want him to, right? I think I know him, too—or I've at least seen him before. I'd remember those soothing blue eyes. Then it hits me: this is another dream with that gorgeous boy in that strange green flower field. I really need to relax and stop watching TV before bed.

Before I know what I'm doing, I answer him. "I've been here only a little while."

He stops right in front of me, just an arm's length away. He smells like fresh-cut grass. "Alexa, it's nearing time to stay." His voice is so comforting and warm, I almost want to believe him.

"Stay where? Who are you, and why do you keep invading my sleep?" I can't help but stare at him. He's beautiful. His milky white skin is unblemished. His slim-fitting blue, button-down shirt match his crystal-blue eyes perfectly, but it's his dark denim, hip-hugging jeans that render me speechless.

He grabs my hand. A frisson of pleasure zips through my body, an icy-hot sensation. It's such a strange yet enjoyable phenomenon. I squeeze his hand back, and we stare at each other for what seems like hours, but in reality, it's only seconds before I notice his hand pulling away.

"My name is Jax. I'll see you again soon." The sides of his mouth lift into a smirk as he continues to speak. I can see his lips move, but I can no longer hear anything.

"What? I can't hear you," I shout, but he doesn't respond. I so badly want to talk to him. I long to ask him why I keep dreaming about him and this magical place.

Too late. I watch as his once solid, muscular body becomes transparent. What's he saying? I peer behind me and see the trees lining the field evaporate one by one. I'm being pulled from my reverie. The smell of lilacs is changing into the smell of coffee.

"Alexa, are you up?" My mom's voice drifts into my subconscious and drags me out of my fantasy world. I open my eyes to see my Lady Gaga poster staring back at me.

"I'm up, Mom!" I jump out of bed and grab a towel. That dream turned out to be even crazier than last time. Jax is such a weird name. And his eyes—incredibly striking, unlike any color I've ever seen before.

"Stop, Alexa, it's just a dream," I remind myself out loud. "Get ready to face the day."

Today is Friday, and Michael will be walking me to school again. Since our study session on Monday, he has walked me to and from school every day this week. He chaperones me to class and eats lunch with me. This week has me thinking that just maybe school *is* enjoyable. I smile and start to sing in the shower.

I only wish that Sheri would return one of my ten phone calls this week. I'm not sure why she's avoiding me. She cancelled on me, and then I never heard from her again. I know she celebrated her birthday last weekend. Could she still be busy? I try not to dwell on it and chalk it up to her having a serious boyfriend. Now that I'm spending more time with Michael, I can certainly see how that might happen to a girl.

When I finally enter the kitchen, my mom hits me with the same question as usual: "What do you want for breakfast, Alexa?"

"I'll make toast, Mom. Don't worry." I feel bad that my mom is always trying to feed me. I don't want to be rude, but I'll be seventeen, and I don't think other kids my age still have their mothers making them meals.

"What kind of breakfast is that? It's not very nutritious. You do know that it's the most important meal of the day?" She sighs and continues to drink her coffee while skimming the newspaper.

"How can I forget, Mom, when you're always reminding me?" I shoot back with a sardonic smile.

Ignoring my comment, she puts down the newspaper and scrutinizes me with a level, concerned stare. "I'm working the night shift tonight, but I'll be home in time for your big birthday breakfast tomorrow morning. We have so much to do tomorrow. But if you want, I can try to find coverage so I'm home with you tonight."

"No, that's fine, Mom. I'm just going to come home and do homework and maybe watch a movie." I butter my toast and sit down at the counter next to her. "Do you mind if I'm not here tomorrow night for my birthday? I'm thinking of going to the homecoming dance."

"You mean at the *school*?" Mom gawks in surprise, probably because I'm talking about going to a school event that isn't mandatory.

"I was just thinking about it, Mom. I haven't really decided yet." I'm sure she can tell by my defensive reaction that I indeed have made up my mind to attend, but I don't want to talk about it.

"Does this have anything to do with that cute boy you were studying with the other day?" she asks slyly. "You know, the one you've been walking to school with every day this week?"

I lower my gaze to the granite countertop to hide my embarrassment and blushing face. Something about him makes my stomach do somersaults, but I don't want her to know that—she's my mom! "Mom, he asked me, but I'm only *thinking* of saying yes. I'm not sure yet." I pause and peek up at her to gauge her reaction. "Sheri was going to come visit for the weekend, but she texted me earlier in the week and cancelled because she has a family obligation. I haven't been able to reach her since."

The smirk spreads across her face and I know she's happy, not only because I'll be venturing out of the house on a weekend, but also because it'll be with someone besides her or Sheri.

I have to admit, at first I was disappointed about Sheri not making the time to come visit me, but not anymore. My heart beat speeds up thinking about going to the dance with Michael. Hopefully, Sheri can come visit for a weekend soon and I can fill her in on my date. Maybe we will both have boyfriends at the same time. The thought makes me squirm with excitement.

"Okay, no problem," Mom says. "It's your birthday, so do whatever you want to do. The only thing I insist on is a big birthday breakfast with me. Then we can go last-minute dress shopping for the big dance."

I can see my mother trying to hide her smug grin behind the paper. She loves shopping, especially with me—and for me. I'm not a fan, but I do need a dress to wear. "That sounds great, Mom. Thank you." I give her a kiss on the cheek and head toward the door. I can sense Michael will be here any minute.

"Alexa, don't worry about Sheri. I'm sure she's busy with school," Mom suddenly says. "I heard from her mom this week and Sheri got a job, so currently she's juggling a lot." Her gregarious grin reassures me. Maybe Sheri is simply just busy and not ignoring me.

Just as I open the front door, I see him strolling up the walkway. The combination of Beiber hair and his warm, friendly demeanor sends a wave of excitement through me. My boring life is really turning around. The only thing I have to get under control is my crazy dreams.

Michael's eyes meet mine and he walks right over to me and grabs my math book. *How chivalrous*, I think with a contented grin.

"Thanks, Michael." I push the image of Jax from my mind as I shut the front door.

After American Government class, I quickly run to my locker to put my books away and pick up the ones I need for after lunch. As soon as I open my locker, I know someone has been in it. My books have been moved and my notebooks are no longer lined up by my schedule.

Without looking behind me, I can sense someone watching me. I try not to let on that I know someone is there as I put my locker in order and take out the books I need.

I pull out my English folder and a loose paper falls to the floor. I'm the most organized high school student—loose papers are a rarity with me. I bend down and pick up the folded, lined paper and open it.

The handwriting isn't mine. My name and the date at the top are in my handwriting, and I remember writing those, then drifting off in class, reliving my dreams. There's something else written there, but it's barely legible. I flip the paper over to see if there are any other marks. Nothing.

I turn it back over and sideways until I can barely make out the chicken scratching: *He's not who you think he is.*

I blink several times to make sure what I'm seeing is actually there. That paper could be for anyone, I tell myself. It probably got mixed up in a handout and I put it in my folder by accident. Nervously, I push the paper deep into my bag and shut my locker. I spin around, half expecting to catch someone behind me, but no one is there. Could I be losing my mind? I walk briskly to lunch because, at the very least, I'm spooked.

Where did that paper come from? Who was in my locker?

As I near the cafeteria, I can smell milk and reheated pizza. The grotesque yet familiar aromas calm my nerves. I pass by the hot-lunch line and find a table. I decide to forget about the note for now and try to enjoy lunch.

I jump in line for the salad bar. I'm so happy they added this new menu item this year. The salad bar is all anyone talked about toward the end of last year. The fresh food is popular. Even though the line is always long, it beats the alternative choices. I'm lucky I'm running late today; the line is short now.

Lunchtime is always my favorite time for people watching. I love to observe as Mandy's friends flock to her, yet I can't help but wonder why she's so popular. It definitely can't be her grades. Last year, she barely got out of the tenth grade. But everyone seems to love her. I bet that gorgeous boy from my dream would love her, too.

Why can't I stop thinking about him? Michael has been so great. Why would I waste my time thinking about a dream? No need to fixate on an illusion, I remind myself. I actually have a real date to mentally prepare myself for.

"Hi, Alexa." Michael startles me as he pulls up his lunch tray next to mine.

Relieved, I welcome his good-looking distraction. "Hey, ready for the big test this afternoon?" I ask.

"Not really. But I'm more confident since we studied the other day. Thanks for that." Michael smiles warmly.

"No problem. I'll study with you anytime."

His big, brown eyes catch mine and my face instantly flushes. "Alexa, you seem distant. Is everything okay?"

"Oh, I'm fine. Just thinking about the test," I lie. I don't want to share with him that I've been dreaming about an unusual, imaginary place where a hot, blue-eyed boy watches me. Or that someone left a cryptic note in my locker. I think for sure I would sound a bit crazy.

We both start eating our lunch, talking about the latest high school gossip. Apparently, Mandy is having boyfriend problems and is going to the dance solo. Strangely, I find comfort knowing that her life isn't as perfect as it appears. Sometimes I wish I could be her, or at least friends with her. She always seems so put together, and her life is definitely more exciting than mine. She's popular, has great hair, and is captain of the cheerleading squad—all while in tenth grade, which amazes me. Mandy appears so natural, like she was born to be the girl with everything—or so I thought before the news of her boyfriend issues.

The lunch bell rings and, like clockwork, the tables empty and the line forms heading out of the cafeteria. As we filter into line, Michael puts his hand in mine and we walk silently to my class. He doesn't take his hand from mine until we reach my classroom door. Then, with an ear-to-ear smile, he continues on to his class. I linger in the hall a few moments, watching him walk to class.

Just as I spin around, a dark figure dashes behind the school announcement wall. I know someone had just been there because the fluorescent-green fliers pinned to it are dancing in the air. I wait a few seconds before walking toward the wall.

With each step closer, my heart bangs harder and harder against my chest. My head turns side to side, scanning for any nearby students or faculty. But it's oddly quiet. The bell has already rung and everyone is in class.

My heart races faster and faster, but I keep moving forward. One more step and I'll be able to peek around the corner.

"Ms. Jenkinson, what do you think you're doing out of class?" The sound of my name makes me jump. I whirl around to see Mr. Riley approaching me.

"Um...um...I thought I dropped something on the way back from lunch. I'm just retracing my steps to find it." I glance up at him, trying to hide my embarrassment, but my hot cheeks are probably giving me away.

"Ms. Jenkinson, it's imperative that you're in class at the bell. Now hurry along. Whatever you may have dropped will be at Lost and Found at the end of the day." While staring me down, his eyes seem to instantly darken. One on one with Mr. Riley is completely unnerving. "Run along to class—and you'd better not be late to your exam this afternoon, or there will be consequences." His voice is commanding and emotionless. Before I can respond, he's off.

I take a few deep breaths and walk back to my class. I try to focus on the fact that I only have two classes left before my big weekend—English class and Mr. Riley's biology test.

My birthday weekend is only hours away. I still can't believe I'm going to my first school semi-formal dance with Michael tomorrow. Thinking of him twirling me around the dance floor slows my heart rate.

I hope I'm not getting my hopes up for nothing. Who knows, maybe I can be the average high school girl who gets involved in extracurricular activities and has a social life. Perhaps I can even acquire a boyfriend, specifically the one who is cherished by the popular clique.

I smile. The thought of Michael becoming my boyfriend thrills me, and it makes waiting for the weekend even more difficult. It also helps me to forget about the strange locker break-in and my awkward encounter with Mr. Riley.

I open the door to my English classroom and find an empty seat in the back so I can secretly review for my biology test next period. I wouldn't want to do poorly and get Mr. Riley upset. He's a little frightening, and I don't want to disappoint him.

Four

"PUMALIA IS THE NAME of this place, in case you're wondering." Jax says it matter-of-factly, as if I know where I am.

"Pumalia? I just want to wake up. Why do I keep coming here?"

He scrunches his eyebrows, creating creases in his perfect forehead. He clearly thinks I'm peculiar. But I'm used to that. "You're supposed to be here. You were born here. You came here last night, and the night before. Don't you remember?"

"What do you mean, I was born here?" My palms start to sweat. I try to take a deep breath, but I can't. Panic settles deep within and all I want is to wake up. I know I'm just dreaming; I'm not *here*, or anywhere. "I'm obviously dreaming, as usual."

"No one has told you yet?" His voice rises in pitch and I can tell he's confused. "You're a half-breed. All half-breeds come home at the human age of seventeen. Elena hasn't mentioned this fact?"

"Elena? Are you talking about my mother?" How did he know my mom's name?

He tenses up. "Yes. She isn't really your mother. She is your guardian, sent to watch over you."

This is too much to be believable. "Okay, so you're telling me that my mother isn't my mother, and I'm a half-breed from Puma-whatever-it-is?" I laugh. Hysterically. I occasionally do that when I get nervous. "And I'm 'home'?" Despite my skepticism, worry flushes over me as I entertain his crazy notions. "Oh, yes, and Elena is my guardian. If that is true, then where are my real parents? This is absurd. You're crazy!"

"It's actually Pumalia, not Puma. I'm not sure why you keep coming here. Your birthday is tomorrow, and at that point, the dreamlike state that you believe you are in becomes more frequent. Typically, the one being reintroduced to Pumalia knows at this point what's going to happen during their transition. However, you still have no idea who you really are?" Avoiding eye contact with me, he places his hands in the pockets of his jeans.

Could this be true? My life isn't what it seems? That's impossible. I cling to the fact that this dream will soon be over and I can return to some normalcy. "That's not funny. How do you know it's my birthday tomorrow?"

"Once again, Alexa, you must wait. I can't answer these questions. I shouldn't have told you as much as I have."

I can tell he feels bad, though not enough to admit to this horrible prank. I clench my fists and my body rocks. I get right in his face. "Jax, right? Let me tell you something. This sick, twisted game is over. Take me home, wake me up, do whatever it is that you do to make me go back to my life. I've heard enough."

He shifts his stance and clears his throat, obviously uncomfortable. "It's not that easy."

"What do you mean, it's not that easy?"

"A half-breed is a being from two different planets. We call all alien or different life forms 'beings.' Alexa, right now, you have the ability to come and go through your dreams as often as you want. When a half-breed turns seventeen, it's no longer safe to go back and forth from your human life to your Pumalian life—in fact, it's forbidden. Laws have been created to prohibit travel to and from Earth and other planets. Because you're still dreaming, you can wake up whenever you want. However, tomorrow this will change."

He clearly knows what he's talking about, even if he does sound ridiculous. His confident demeanor and knowledge make me wonder if this crazy story is actually true. What does he mean when he says "safe"? Earth isn't safe? I've lived here all my life. I have a dance to go to tomorrow night, not some stupid make-believe planet. Can I wake up, already?

I realize it's almost time to wake up, because he's beginning to disappear. I glance behind me. The tree-lined field is also dissolving. Quickly, I peer back at Jax and he offers me a wave and a small smile just before he vanishes.

I know I'm next. I gaze down at my hands and can see the ground through them. Soon, I'll be awake and trying to make sense of this nightmare.

As my eyes snap open, I find myself face to face with the cat. I search my surroundings to ensure I'm in my bed. These dreams make me wonder if I'm losing my mind.

I quickly jump out of bed and glance at the calendar on my wall. "Today's the day," I crow. "Not only is it my birthday, but the homecoming dance is tonight." Excitement grows in the pit of my stomach, swirling and tickling my insides.

My excitement plummets when I see the time: 11:00 a.m. My mother hasn't come in to wake me for my annual birthday-bash breakfast? Maybe she wants me to be well rested for my big night.

Usually by now, the smells of my birthday breakfast feast should be wafting into my bedroom, but I don't smell any pancakes, bacon, or sausage. I grab my sweatshirt and throw it on, then fly down the stairs, ready to lay the guilt trip on my mother for not preparing my birthday breakfast.

Silence greets me at the bottom of the stairs. No food, no coffee, nothing. It's all too quiet and extremely odd. I search in the family room and my mom's bedroom, but she's nowhere. I peek into the garage, only to see her parked car there, as usual.

Maybe she got a call and had to rush into work, and maybe she was picked up? I search for a note on the counter. Nothing. Very strange. I pick up the house phone and dial her cell phone. The ringing goes right through to her voicemail. I notice her blue-and-white, polka-dot purse sitting in its usual place on the counter. Everything indicates she's here, but she isn't.

This is crazy.

Maybe I should call the police. No. "Okay, relax, Alexa," I admonish myself. "She probably went running or for a walk. That's why her stuff is here and she isn't." For a moment, the thought comforts me. Even though I don't really believe it.

I force myself to walk back upstairs to take a shower. Scary scenarios play in my mind as I squeeze the banister. With each step, I picture her in danger or hurt.

"Alexa, stop this craziness," I murmur out loud. "You can't be thinking like this. You'll take a shower, and by the time you get out, she'll be home."

I grab a nice, fluffy, brown towel from the linen closet and turn on the shower. I step in and the hot water rinses away my worried thoughts.

These weird, night-after-night dreams are really messing with my psyche. Dreaming of strange places isn't a foreign idea for me, but I always thought of it more like a fairytale rather than an actual dream.

When I close my eyes in an effort to wash away my latest dream, Jax's mysteriously enchanting blue eyes and pouty lips pop into my mind. I slowly rinse the conditioner out of my hair and make a silent agreement with myself to stop thinking about a make-believe person, even if he is gorgeous.

Opening my eyes, I try to focus on the real problem. Where is my mother? I need to believe that when I get out of the shower, she'll be downstairs concocting enough breakfast for five, as usual.

I hear something downstairs when I step out of the shower—footsteps and dishes clanking together. I smile. I bet she's whipping up my breakfast. She's definitely down there doing something. Relief washes over me. How silly I was to worry.

I quickly towel-dry my hair and throw on my favorite gray sweatpants and matching pink and gray hoodie. I wonder where we will be shopping today. I need to find the perfect dress for the dance tonight.

"Mom!" No answer.

She probably can't hear me because she's throwing in laundry. I toss my towel on the bathroom floor and bolt down the stairs. No breakfast cooking, still no coffee prepared. This is so strange. I know I heard her down here.

I head for the living room, hoping to see her reading the morning newspaper on the leather love seat. As I turn the corner from the kitchen into the living room, I see him.

I blink a few times, not believing that what I see is real. My heart starts to pound in my chest and a warm numbness crawls up my neck. I must be dreaming. How can *he* be here?

My body trembles and my stomach tenses and I struggle for air. My mouth becomes dry and I know what's going to happen next. Black spots enter my peripheral vision—and that's the last thing I can see.

I try to blink the dark spots away, but it doesn't work. "What did you do to my mother?" My voice is unsteady and small, but I'm sure he heard me.

My ears start to ring and I know I can't prevent the inevitable. I listen to my heartbeat in my ears and attempt to linger, but my conscious moments are dwindling. My knees buckle. I slowly fold down like an accordion and everything goes black.

Five

"ALEXA! ALEXA, WAKE UP!" His voice drops to a mutter. "I can't believe she fainted. This is why we integrate slowly and guide them through the transition." He sighs in frustration and I can sense him rising, moving away from me. "This would never have happened, had she been treated like all other half-breeds."

I can hear Jax as he paces in the kitchen beside me. I can hear everything he's saying, but I'm not ready to open my eyes because none of this makes sense. I'm not ready for this.

His footsteps pause beside me. "Can you hear me, Alexa?"

He's pacing again. "I knew she was in the bathroom. How else could I let her know I was here without scaring her?"

I want to laugh because he's in a full-blown conversation with himself.

He pauses again. His voice turns thoughtful. "Her skin is paler in person. When she teleports, she appears darker. And taller."

"I can hear you." I blink my eyelids multiple times, squinting, preparing for the rush of light. I can't let him go on about me while I listen. It's embarrassing.

He drops to his knees beside me. "Alexa, are you okay? How is your head?" he anxiously asks. "You bumped it on the floor when you fell."

Instantly, I bring my hand to my head and wince in pain. He watches, his face a mixture of concern and relief. He probably thought he'd killed me. Or maybe he hoped he had.

"Are you okay?"

"Am I dreaming?" I wonder out loud.

"No," he murmurs.

"I believe you were saying something about how I appear shorter in person," I say archly. "What's that supposed to mean?"

"Well, it isn't anything bad, but ninety percent of the time, teleports appear exactly the same everywhere. Looking at you now, I notice you appear different, here on Earth. You're still beautiful," he adds, "but you appear somewhat more delicate."

"Oh, okay, I thought you were calling me short. Now I'm beautiful?" Half of me wants him to say it again, but I don't give him the chance to disappoint me, so I quickly ask, "Why are you here, anyway? What did you do with my mother?"

"Alexa, do you remember my name?" I sit up slowly and Jax reaches across and touches my hand. As soon as he does, I pull back. "I'm not going to hurt you. Please don't be scared."

"I'm not dreaming?"

"No, you're not dreaming. However, we've met in your dreams. You have been teleporting frequently to Pumalia. Do you remember any of those visits?" he asks.

"Yes." My face flushes as I recall all the moments I've daydreamed about him and his gorgeous physique.

"Okay. So you know my name and who or what you are?"

"Your name is Jax. You claim to live on a faraway planet. You also told me that I would live there as well because I belong there. But all that was a dream and now I'm awake and you're in my home." I try to reply with little to no sarcasm, but I can't help myself. It comes out in a skeptical, singsong tone.

He sits back. "Are you always this rude? Or are you making a special exception for me?"

"I'm not being rude. I'm just irritated. Everything is so confusing and I really can't tell if I'm dreaming or if this is for real," I admit.

He sighs. "Okay, let's start over. All of what I've told you is true. We must leave now—it's time for you to go home."

I stand up and search my surroundings only to see that my house appears the same. Surprisingly, nothing is moved or altered. The only thing obviously different is that my mom is still missing and the Greek god from my dream is standing in my kitchen.

"Where is my mother? What did you do with her?" Panic runs through me. Something isn't right. An uneasy sense stalks through my body, leaving me sick to my stomach. He comes off as being kind and helpful, but maybe he did something to her.

"Alexa, please trust me. She's okay, and we will see her once we get back. Your guardian has already been picked up. We really need to leave. I want you to trust me and come with me of your own accord. But if it comes down to it, I'll drug you with medication and drag you out of here."

He'll drug me? Who does this jerk think he is? I can't believe I thought he was attractive. "I'm sleeping, I'm sleeping, I'm sleeping..." I spin around and stare at him directly in the eyes. "Do you know where my mother is?"

"Yes."

"Take me to her." I respond with clenched teeth. Before he can comment, I pivot and head for the door. I need to stay calm and find her before I lose my nerve.

One minute I'm dreaming, the next thing I know, I'm awake and my dreams have followed me into the real world. Why does he keep staring at me like that? It's my birthday; I'm going to a dance tonight. I'm going to do normal, fun, teenager things. This can't be happening right now.

I feel nervous leaving the house because a large part of me is waiting to wake up to the sound of my mother singing happy birthday in her usual off-key, soprano voice.

"Jax, how are we going to get to my mother? If she's on Puma or whatever you call it, are we going to go there, too?" That must have been a stupid question because I can see the corners of his mouth starting to curve upward in a smart-ass smirk. "Are my questions entertaining you?" I don't give him time to respond. "I would appreciate some answers. I at least deserve that."

"Yes, we're going to Pumalia. Your guardian is there. To see her, we need to get in the starship and go."

Now it's my turn to laugh. "I'm sorry, did you say starship?"

Jax points across the street to a silver car that looks a lot like my neighbor's ordinary, four-door sedan. I follow him toward it, expecting to wake up at any moment.

"Okay, so we're driving there in a car. You should have just said that." This will be interesting. We're taking the starship-sedan to find my mom on a different planet. "How long is this going to take? I have plans for tonight."

"Clearly, you don't understand, Alexa. You don't belong here. You're not from here. You're going home. Haven't you ever felt out of place here?"

His words resonate. I start to think maybe he isn't all that crazy. Maybe this place we are going to *is* my home.

"Jax, I need to at least tell my date Michael I won't be going to the dance with him tonight. I don't want him to think I stood him up." I'm not sure how I feel about that. How will I be able to explain this to him? I need to find my mom, but I can't simply call Michael and say, "Hi, I'm being abducted by aliens and I hope to be back later for the dance, but I'm not sure." He definitely won't ever talk to me again if I do that.

"Okay, why don't you just text him and tell him you're ill? He won't remember you after tomorrow, anyway." As soon as the words come out of his mouth, his eyes widen and he squeezes his lips together—he realizes he has made a mistake. He's right.

"What?" My breathing becomes labored and I feel as if I'll black out again.

"Alexa, I'm sorry to throw all of this at you, but we really have to go, and quickly. Everything will be explained to you, I promise." He does seem sympathetic, but I could be dreaming, I remind myself. Or he could be a serial killer.

Either way, I have to get my mom back. I follow Jax across the street to the silver car. He opens my door first. "What a gentlemen," I drawl. "You can open my car door, but you couldn't knock on the front door this morning?" He didn't answer and I didn't expect him to. I could tell I was aggravating him.

Inside, I'm unsurprised by how much the interior resembles a standard car. There's a steering column and a wheel, though it's a smaller-than-standard version. The dashboard lights are orange and the seats are black bucket seats like those in my mom's Honda Accord. So far, I'm not impressed with this so-called journey to Pumalia in the starship.

His eyes twinkle and I'm transfixed. "We're almost ready; put on your safety belt." I reach my right hand up to retrieve my belt, but it's not there. Jax reaches across me, his tan, muscular arm skimming against my chest. Chills run up my arms and my face heats, but before I can truly be embarrassed by my reaction, my seat attacks me.

"What was that?" I shriek. "You could have warned me."

"That's a safety harness. We will be traveling at light speed and it's important that you're secure in your seat." He can't help but grin at my outburst. His playful smugness is annoying.

All I really want to do is break into laughter. He is so serious, talking about safety in this car that resembles any other normal sedan on the street. "This starship is a lot like my neighbor's Nissan Sentra. How are we going to get to some planet in this?" I roll my eyes at him and watch as he presses his own button on the door that releases a harness from his seat.

He adjusts some gauges and buttons on the dash and I wait for something big. A big takeoff, an explosion, something—but instead we just roll on down my little lonely street.

"We might not have a lot of time. We need to do this before someone sees us. Hold onto the door, Alexa. We have to move fast. I don't normally take off in the daytime. And for the record, this isn't an ordinary car. It's a starship. And once again, it travels at the speed of light, so hold on."

"Okay...whatever you say." I grab the shiny, silver bar on the door.

The car comes to an abrupt stop on Garfield Street. I thought we had to move fast; what happened? I turn to Jax and watch as a sly grin spreads across his face. I know he has something in store for me. I'm just not sure what it is.

"Wait, I need to tell Michael I won't be able to go to the dance. I almost forgot." I pull my phone from my pocket and quickly text: *Hi Michael! I can't make it to the dance tonight. I'm not feeling well. I'll see you at school Monday. – Alexa.* I hit Send and try to ignore the pang of guilt that strikes. I really hate to lie to him.

"Sit back, Alexa." Jax opens a compartment in the center of the dashboard and punches a few numbers on the green glowing keypad. As soon as he hits Enter, my whole body slams back into the seat. I grip the handle more firmly and watch out the window as my street and house get smaller and smaller until they're the size of a speck of sand. The starship is taking us straight up at a dizzying speed. We quickly enter and emerge above fluffy white clouds.

My mouth drops open as the floor beneath me transforms from a metal floor into a window that stretches from one end of the car to the other. A vast, open blackness envelops us as I watch the white fluffy clouds disappear.

When I peer down below me, I see Earth, the way it's depicted in my textbooks from school. It's simply beautiful, a perfect combination of green and blue. Excitement grips the pit of my stomach, as if I'm on a crazy roller coaster ride. What's going to happen next? I take a peek over at Jax and he appears cool, calm, and collected.

He swings his gaze back to me and winks. "Are you impressed by this 'typical car' yet?" He grins when I work my mouth, but no sound comes out. How can I possibly answer him when what I'm seeing has left me awestruck?

"Get ready, we're taking off." Jax enters more numbers on the green pad in front of him.

"But aren't we already flying?" I manage.

"We only went up, now we must move forward. Make sure you hold on tight."

I don't second-guess Jax this time. I grab onto the sides of the seat and brace myself for forward movement.

Loud noises from the engine warn me that at any moment we will be moving. I press my head back into the seat. Averting my eyes, I take one last glance out the window at Earth. I wonder if I'll ever be coming back—part of me also wonders if I'd ever want to come back.

My thoughts are disrupted when my body is thrust back into my seat. Neon lights blur past us. I close my eyes and focus on the task at hand.

Finding my mom.

Six

"ALEXA, ARE YOU ALL right? You've been really quiet since takeoff."

I can hear Jax talking to me, but I really can't think about answering him. My mind is too busy racing through all of the recent events. Part of me feels crazy for even entertaining the idea that this isn't a dream. I wish I could talk to Sheri and tell her about this bizarre mess I'm in. She most likely wouldn't believe me.

"Alexa?"

"I'm okay," I answer, hoping he will let me have some quiet time.

I myself am having a hard time believing this is real. I hope Michael isn't mad at me. I truly wanted to go to the dance with him. I just wanted to go to the mall with my mom and shop for a dress, as normal teenagers do. Now I don't know if I'll ever see her again. That thought alone churns my stomach and bile builds in my throat.

"I don't know why, Alexa, but I don't believe you," Jax says, shooting me a wry glance.

"I'm fine. I'm just wondering when I'll wake up from this nightmare."

"I know this is hard to believe, but once you get there and are integrated, it will all start to make sense. I promise. I know you have no reason to trust me, but you should." He smiles and it almost makes me feel better. But it doesn't.

"Just tell me, Jax—tell me something about this place that I supposedly belong to, please," I quietly plead.

"Sure, ask me a question and I'll answer it."

"Well, if I'm from Pumalia, why haven't I always lived there?"

"Well, when a Pumalian conceives a child with another extraterrestrial from another planet, the child must live on Earth, a neutral place, until he or she turns seventeen years old." I can't help realizing that if this is true, I have two parents, not just one, who are aliens. I think I'm losing my mind—the longer we fly through space, the more I think this could really be happening.

"Are you telling me that my so-called parents are from different planets?" I ask, stupefied by this revelation.

"Yes, much like the Milky Way galaxy, where Earth is found, Pumalia is in our own galaxy, Magna, along with a number of other planets."

"Why have I never heard of the Magna galaxy?" I ask.

Jax gazes over at me and smiles. "Magna is fifty-seven billion light years away from Earth. Earth is still relatively new, and the technology needed to see or to travel that distance has not yet been created."

I'm quiet for a few minutes, pretending to focus on the instruments in front of me. Maybe if I pretend I'm busy, he won't ask me if I'm okay.

I glance back over to Jax. "How much longer until we arrive?"

"We should be there in about six hours," Jax responds confidently.

Cool tears pool in my eyes. I'm so confused and scared. I turn my head and my body so I'm positioned away from Jax. I don't want him to see me upset. This is going to be the longest six hours of my life.

I pull my legs to my chest and recline my seat. "I'm going to sleep. Wake me when we get there." Even if I don't fall asleep, I can pretend. Anything so I don't have to talk about this crazy situation. I close my eyes and take a few deep breaths. My mind and body give in to my need for rest.

"Alexa, we will be landing soon." I open my eyes and quickly study my surroundings outside the window.

It's just like my dreams. Honeydew-green trees stand high around us. I gaze up through the sunroof to see a magenta sky with three glowing moons. "This place is real," I whisper. The sick feeling within my stomach grows. I'm not dreaming after all.

Right before we land, Jax warns me that people will gape at me because I'm clearly new to Pumalia. He's right. As soon as I disembark the starship, I'm instantly aware of all the eyes watching me. This is no different than Mandy and her crew in the hallways at school. Apparently, the high school mentality is everywhere. I don't know why they're staring at me. What makes me stand out as different?

"What are they gawking at, Jax?" I hiss, furiously tugging my sweatshirt hood up and lowering my head as I wait for a response.

"They just want to see who you are. It isn't bad. Relax and just keep walking." His voice sounds impatient. Of course, I can't tell if he's mad at me or just irritated at the situation.

The path through the city comes to an abrupt halt in front of a set of massive doors set in a stone wall at least five stories high. Jax steps up to the wall beside the doors and does something with his hand. I can't see exactly what he's doing from where I'm standing, but it seems to be a lot of elaborate hand movements. He backs away from the wall and the enormous doors slowly creak open.

"Come on, this is where Elena is." Jax leads the way through the open doors, following another walkway that takes us to a sprawling white house. I count the rows of giant windows—there are ten floors. Some of the windows have bars on them, making the house resemble a prison. A chill shivers through my body as we approach the door on a path bordered with giant green bushes bearing orange flower blossoms the size of my head. Two guards in white uniforms stand watch at the front door. The uniforms have the same insignia on the breasts as the one on the starship we flew here in.

This place has never been in my dreams. I would remember this compound. The only familiar thing besides Jax is the magenta skyline, the honeydew trees, and the three aligned moons.

The suspense is killing me. "Where is she? I want to see her now. And then I want to see who runs this place, and I want some answers."

Jax grits his teeth but says nothing in reply to my demands.

We enter through the front door and follow an unadorned hallway to a large room. "Is she here, Jax?" The decor in the room is simple. They really take the saying "less is more" seriously.

"Yes." I can tell he's holding something back. Maybe he isn't sure. Maybe he has no idea if she's here or not. I want to press him for more information, but part of me fears I won't like the answer.

We pass through that room and enter a huge room—almost a hall—with a long table and plenty of chairs around it. The white walls are adorned with candle sconces and a few pieces of abstract art. The windows are floor to ceiling and the view is spectacular. I turn to appreciate rolling hills that undulate to the horizon, then whirl back as the far wall separates, the two halves sliding aside to allow a line of men to march in. They resemble the guards, but they're carrying weapons and wearing white masks. I quickly close the distance to Jax. He doesn't flinch one bit, which relieves me.

After the last white-clad figure has entered, a white-haired man dressed all in black emerges. His flat, black eyes meet mine and instantly I freeze in place. I want my mother—where is she?

His voice is as disturbing as his appearance. "Take her to the dungeon."

Who is he talking about? It can't be me. I've come here to see my mother.

Jax steps in front of me and at that point, I realize it's me they've come for. I grab his jacket and hold it tight, burying my face in the material. This has to be a nightmare!

"Maddox, what do you think you're doing?" Jax isn't faking it—his voice is quavering and his tense body provides proof that he isn't part of this plan.

"She needs to be locked up for her safety—and ours. She is putting us all in danger by being here."

Locked up? Danger? Maddox must be speaking in some sort of code, because I've no idea what he means. How could I be dangerous to anyone?

"Why did we bring her here, then?" Jax demands in a booming voice. "Why was her guardian, Elena, taken prematurely? Why are we both in the dark still? What haven't you told me?" His whole body convulses with anger as I hide behind him. It's apparent he really doesn't know what's happening.

"Jax, this isn't the time to question my authority," Maddox warns. Glancing to the right, he nods at the guards. They start toward me like a swarm of white wasps. My jaw drops.

Jax puts his hand up and they stop. I'm so confused! Who is in charge here? "Stay where you are, men. I'll take her." His last sentence echoes through my body, leaving me in shock. I nervously tremble as the color drains from my already pale face. The hair around my face clings to the sweat accumulating on my forehead.

He spins around and grabs my hands before I fall. I can see his mouth moving, but I can't hear anything. It's as if he's on mute. *Oh, no, I'm going down again!* My heartbeat quickens, the thumping echoing in my ears. As my legs buckle, Jax catches me. The last thing I remember is Jax's strong arm cradling my head.

I just want to wake up from this horrible nightmare.

"Alexa, Alexa, it's time to wake up." A gentle, unfamiliar voice is calling my name.

I blink my eyes a few times, hoping to see the inside of my bedroom. "Where am I? What happened?" I can hear someone shuffling around beside me. The smell of rubbing alcohol irritates my nose as I try desperately to keep my eyes open. My head is pounding as if someone took a hammer to it.

I slowly shift my gaze to the side and see a woman with long, red hair and porcelain-pale skin. I blink a few more times and notice that her white dress bears the same insignia on the chest as the emblem on the starship. I try to raise my head, but it's so very heavy, and the hammering increases to the point where the pain is debilitating.

"Just lie still, Alexa. You'll be just fine. You fainted and hit your head on the floor. You have a small wound, but it isn't too deep. I've cleaned and bandaged it." Her voice is soft and kind.

I try to move my hands, but they won't move. Panic slinks over me when I notice that they're fastened to the bed with chains, like handcuffs. "Alexa, calm down. You don't want to have another fainting episode. The doctor did give you a mild sedative to help you cope with the situation."

I take a few deep breaths, trying to fathom what she's saying, what it all means. "Where is Jax?"

She combs my hair back from my face with her hand and lays a cold compress on my forehead. Her smile is sympathetic and in some ways familiar.

"He'll be back to check on you again later. He was here most of the night, but you never woke up." She seems nice enough, but why am I chained to the bed?

"Why are these on my wrists?" I hold up my hands as far as I can, and she quickly glances away.

"Maddox said you're dangerous and not to be trusted." She must have seen the surprised look on my face, because before I can say anything, she quickly adds, "Don't worry, Alexa. I think he may be confused, or perhaps there has been a miscommunication along the way. You don't seem one bit dangerous to me. Jax is working to resolve the matter as we speak."

I wish her words comforted me, but they don't. The room is dark and dismal. The air smells of mildew, as if an ominous cloud of it is suspended over me and clinging to my body. When I exhale, the air sticks to my lungs. I just need some clean, fresh air. I close my eyes and hope that when I open them, I'll be at home with Michael, on our way to the dance.

Unfortunately, all I can see when I open my eyes are cranberry-colored, velvet curtains hanging from the windows next to my bed. They dangle there, taunting me, swaying slightly whenever the woman moves.

Meanwhile, I remain chained to the bed.

"Um, is there any way you can open the window? It's so dark and stuffy in here. I need some fresh air. I'm feeling claustrophobic."

She doesn't hesitate at my request. She jumps up and moves the curtain aside. Dust billows into the air as she cranks open the window. The fresh air pours in, allowing me to breathe easily. I can't tell if it's morning or afternoon, but at least the natural light and air clears the musty smell from my nose.

"Thank you. What's your name?"

She turns around and takes a few steps closer to the bed. "My name is Gabriella, but you can call me Gabby. Would you like something to eat or drink?" Her large, green eyes are warm, and looking into them makes me less frightened.

I don't want her to leave me here to fulfill any request, but my mouth is dry. "I'm okay. A little thirsty, but—"

Before I can finish, she's off to the other side of the room. She pours me a cup of water from a crystal pitcher on a counter in the corner of the room, returns, and holds the glass to my mouth, tilting it so I can take a sip.

The water tastes delicious. I must have been really thirsty, because I immediately begin to feel more like myself. The metal taste in my mouth, which I'm sure is blood, subsides, and I'm clearly on the mend.

"Thanks, Gabby."

"Of course, sweetie. Anything else I can get for you?"

Why is she being so nice to me? "How old are you?" I can tell by the pause and the look she gives me that my question surprises her.

"Earth age?" Her question catches me off guard. Is aging different here? She doesn't wait for me to answer. I think my dumbfounded expression is answer enough. "I'm twenty-two years old." She smiles and busies herself with tidying the blankets on the bed. Quickly, she adds, "I think you should nap if you can. The trip was exhausting, and I've a feeling it's not over yet."

I have to ask her one more question, even though the need for rest has begun to plague me. My question sounds barely audible. "Are you from here?"

"Wow, Jax was right. You're an inquisitive one." It takes her a few minutes to answer. "No, I'm not from here. I grew up on Earth, actually. I lived my first seventeen years in California."

So she *is* like me. I've so many questions for her, but my eyelids are growing heavier and heavier.

"Do you know where my mother is?" Why am I so tired? Did they give me another sedative? My lids start to shut and I know that once I succumb to the darkness, I'll no longer be able to see her or hear her answer. I can't explain the sensation pulsing through my body, but I know I only have a few moments before I fall asleep against my will. "Please, Gabby, tell me where she is." I blink multiple times, trying to prolong my descent into my muddled dream world.

"Rest, Alexa, you need it. When you wake up, I promise you'll have more answers." Her smile is the last thing I see before I drift off into a deep slumber.

Seven

PRYING MY EYES OPEN is extremely difficult. Willing them to open isn't enough. The muscles around them work hard, but the lids seem to be stuck together, as if someone applied a strong adhesive glue. After many attempts, I'm finally able to open my right one. When I do, I see *his* beautiful blue pools staring back at me. I blink again and I'm able to free myself from this fitful sleep.

Yes, I confirm that Jax isn't only here next to me, but he's gawking. I can't help but be pleased with this. Even though I'm furious, deep down I know I can't stay mad at this face. I take a minute to enjoy the sight of his beautiful olive skin, muscular body, and blond Adonis hair. I need to move past his Zeus like qualities and remember that he let them lock me up. He even delivered me to them.

"Alexa, are you awake?" He sits on the edge of his chair, anticipating my obvious answer.

"No, I'm still sleeping, can't you tell?" I can't help but snap at him. He took me from my home with false hope that I would reunite with my mother. He never once said I would be locked up for absolutely no reason.

"I know you're mad at me, and you have every right to be. But I honestly had no idea that this was going to happen. I'm sorry, truly I am."

I panic slightly because I'm not sure why I believe his apology so quickly. I really don't want to let him off the hook that easily.

"Well, I'm mad. Take me to my mother—*now*," I bark unapologetically. I can tell by the way he sits back in his chair and lets out a loud sigh that it's probably not going to happen.

I avert my attention and stare down at my wrists and notice they're no longer bound. Maybe this is good news; everything was most likely a misunderstanding. Thank goodness I'm a forgiving person and can forget this brief incarceration.

"I'm sorry, Alexa, but that's going to be impossible. I'm not sure where to even begin." The creases in his forehead become visible, and that makes my heart start to race. He stands and moves closer to my bed. Nervousness makes my palms begin to sweat, both in anticipation of the news, and at his sudden closeness. "Your mother isn't here. She never was."

"Where did they take her? What did you do to her?" My eyes sting, and before I know it, tears are spilling onto my shirt. The thought of not ever seeing her again makes my stomach churn. My mom, the one person I've known my whole life—I can't comprehend the idea of not seeing her. She must be worried and scared for both her and me.

"Alexa, I need you to listen." He sits on the edge of my bed and places his hand over mine. Hot, prickly sparks burst over my hand and surge up my arm. I can see his mouth moving, but I can't hear anything. I look down at our hands, and for a moment, I think I see a flickering purple flame. I pull back quickly and he says nothing. It must be the medication they gave me for my head. It must be making me hallucinate.

Jax lowers his head. "First, Elena isn't your mother. She was assigned to care for you on Earth. She's your guardian, and you'll be able to see her soon."

"What? How can you tell me something like this? Why must you lie to me?" My body starts to tremble with rage. I picture my mom's face and relief floods me. I don't believe anything he says.

"I'm sorry, but it's much more complicated than that. Your birth mother is from another planet in our galaxy, our rival planet, Mapu. Her planet preys on Pumalia and its resources. She's not only from there, she's their leader, the queen."

Jax's voice doesn't waver, and I know his solemn manner is an indication of how dire the situation is. But I throw my head back and laugh. My face is noticeably stiff from the tears moments ago, and that makes me laugh even more. I can't believe this. First, I'm a half-breed in transition, or something like that. Now I'm from a different planet? My mom is a queen from a rival planet?

He has to be mistaken.

But his blank expression says it all. The more I laugh, the more I realize this is most likely my new reality. "So, Jax, let me get this story straight. My mother, who has raised me since I can remember, is a wicked queen from yet another planet? Do you think I'm that gullible?" My body stiffens as I wait for an answer.

"Alexa, the woman living with you was never your mother. You were placed on Earth, as all half-breeds are."

"So where is Elena, my Earth mother? Also, how am I a Pumalian half-breed if my mother isn't even from this planet?"

"Elena is debriefing her assignment. When she's done, I'll try to get her in here. I'm sorry, Alexa. I can't tell you any more right now. I can't imagine what you're feeling. I wish there was something I could do or say to make it better."

"There is: let me go. I want to go back to my life. If I'm not a typical being, let me live my Earth life. I was just getting the hang of it." Anger brews deep down in the pit of my stomach, sour, vile. I can't believe I've been taken to this ridiculous place and fed this incredibly far-fetched story. The worst part is that Jax seems to believe it, too. I'm going to have to figure out my own plan.

"It's not that easy, Alexa. I wish I could. Maddox has filled me in and he won't let you leave here. He agreed to take off the chains, but I promised him you wouldn't run. There's nowhere to go, anyway. We have to figure this out here. It's possible your *real* mother has started looking for you. Her people are very dangerous, and to remain safe, you need to be here." Jax lets out a huge sigh and rises from the bed. He paces at its foot for a few minutes. Neither of us say a word.

"Does my mother want to kill me?" That sounds absurd. Why can't I go to her? None of this is making any sense to me. I bet she could explain it all much better.

He slowly moves over to the bed and places his hand on mine. The now familiar electrifying sensation creeps up my arm and down my spine. I quickly jerk my hand away. He appears to be upset that I'm so unhappy.

"I wouldn't say she wants to kill you, but she isn't known for her endearing qualities. I'm not comfortable suggesting that she would harm you. But that's not the point. Unfortunately, your father isn't here to ask. He was killed by her people a number of years ago."

"My father?" I begin to feel lightheaded and a tad woozy. I always thought my father's death was an accident. Elena told me so. Never once did I think he was alive while I was growing up in my urban neighborhood with my fake mom. Why would my "real" mother murder him? Who is this woman? I still can't help but think this is a misunderstanding or a prolonged, awkward dream.

A knock at the door disturbs the images flying around in my head.

"Who is it?" Jax stands against the door, waiting for a reply.

"It's Gabby. I have breakfast for Ms. Jenkinson." The idea of food excites my body and my mouth begins to water. I can't remember the last time I ate something.

"Come in, Gabby." Jax opens the door. "I was just getting ready to leave. If you need anything, Alexa, there are two guards stationed outside your door. They both know how to reach me."

Gabby answers before I can offer a snide remark. "Thank you, Jax. I'll make sure she has whatever she needs."

I watch his body tense as he approaches the doorway and walks out. The door shuts quickly behind him before I can glimpse what lies beyond it.

Gabby brings the tray over to the table by the window and takes off the cover. The smell of pancakes and bacon make me dizzy. The thought of eating consumes me, and without hesitation, I jump up for breakfast.

"Stop, I don't know why I'm here! Please don't hurt me." She tightens her grip on my wrist and pulls me toward her glowing, orange eyes. All I can see are cement walls and bars on the windows. I struggle, and she squeezes my wrist harder. I stare into her eyes and she flings back her head and lets out a rolling laugh.

"You don't tell me what to do," she declares. "I'm the queen, and I'm your mother."

"There must be a mistake. I'm not who you think I am." I tremble within her clutches.

"No, there's no mistake, Alexa. You were taken from me. Hidden from me. Now you're mine, all mine." I gape at her evil smile and know this is a nightmare. A mother would never say these things to her child.

"Please, let go, you're hurting me," I sob. Tears stream down my face. "I'll do whatever you need me to do. Just please, let go."

Her grip loosens and I back away from her. I stare down at my wrist. The skin is burned in an angry-red shade.

"I've been searching for you for quite some time." Her voice drips with malice. Wavy, dark hair sways from side to side as she scrutinizes me up and down.

She takes another step toward me. I take one back. The cool cement wall presses along my spine. I'm trapped. Nowhere to go. I close my eyes, hoping that when I open them, I'll be somewhere else, anywhere else.

She creeps closer and I squeeze my eyes more tightly shut.

"Alexa, Alexa wake up!"

Someone is screaming my name, but I can't tell if it's in my dream or in real life. Both worlds seem to keep merging and blurring my sense of reality.

"Alexa, you were dreaming. You're perfectly safe. Open your eyes."

I know that voice. It's Jax. I slowly pry my eyes open, allowing them to adjust to the light. I blink a few times before focusing on my handsome captor. "What're you doing here?" My words are biting—I wouldn't be stuck in here if it weren't for him.

"I came to check on you. When I got to the hallway outside your door, I could hear you screaming."

"What do you care what happens to me?" I reply sharply, longing to hurt him in some way.

Completely avoiding my question, he presses on with his own. "What were you dreaming of?"

Why is he acting like he cares? Why hasn't he freed me from this place? "It doesn't matter, I'm awake now and chained to the bed again, as if I'm a convict," I mutter. I raise my voice and try to sound stern, but my words fracture with emotion. "Please, just let me go!"

"It's not me, Alexa. You know I would if I could, but Maddox said it was for your own good. He told me just a few more days, and all of this will be cleared up. He did agree to allow Elena, your Earth mother, to come in and sit with you today."

Tears sting the corners of my eyes. "She was here? But I wanted to see her." I make a frustrated growling noise from deep in my throat. "Why can't you just take me home? I just want to wake up." I close my eyes and wish with all my might that when I open them, I'll be home in my room.

"I'm truly sorry, Alexa. I promise, I had no idea this would happen. If I'd known, I would have done things differently." Jax touches my arm, which jolts my eyes open. He jerks his hand away, but my skin still remains warm where he touched me. The sensation moves up my arm, sending an electrical pulse through my body.

"Did you feel that?" He stares at me with an intensity that makes me shift my gaze away from him. Unable to resist the urge, I glance back. He examines his hands, seeming to search for evidence that something happened.

"Please, just go away," I mumble. "I want to be alone."

"If that's what you want. I'll send Gabby back in, and Elena, as soon as she arrives." I don't watch him leave, but I hear the heavy door open and his footsteps fade down the hall.

"How do I get out of here?" I whisper. I'm lying on my back. I stare up at the cracked ceiling. "I need a plan, and fast," I whisper to myself. But my mind drifts, and darkness surrounds me.

Eight

A KNOCK ON THE DOOR startles me. "Alexa, are you okay?" I hear her voice before I see her face and I can't believe my eyes. Mom. She quickly makes her way to the bed I'm secured to.

"Is that really you?" I whisper.

She nods with a half-grin. "Of course it is."

It *is* her! My mom's soft, comforting touch on my forehead as her hand brushes the hair away from my face is unmistakable. I flutter my swollen eyelids, squint at her. "Is this real?" I can't believe she's actually here, staring back at me. This has to be some cruel joke, or a dream that I can't shake. "Are you really here?" My voice starts to tremble, and then come the waterworks.

"Please, don't cry, Alexa. I need you to listen. We don't have much time, and there's a lot I need to tell you." Elena strips the restraints away from my wrists and tosses them on the bed. I quickly scan the room looking for Gabby, but oddly, she isn't where she usually is. I notice that Elena appears different—more serious, and even older. I can tell she's upset and that I have to calm down and pay attention.

"Okay." I can't just turn off the tears. But I want to know what's happening and how to get out of here.

Mom takes a deep breath. "I'm not sure what they told you, but let me start at the beginning. And like I said before, I don't have much time, so you must be strong and really listen to me.

"I have cared for you from the time you were born, until the day they took me away from you. I feel that you're my very own daughter." Her lips tremble as she spills this truth. "You must know, Alexa, even though I'm not your birth mother, I love you like you're my own daughter. I've always wanted to keep you safe. I never thought this would happen. I didn't know that they knew where we were. That's why I must be honest with you now.

"Your father is a great man. He entrusted you to me. They will try to tell you otherwise, but don't listen. Your father is a powerful man, and Maddox is threatened. That's partly why you're locked in here."

Her eyes fill with tears. She takes another deep breath and continues talking, but all I hear is "your father." I start to quake with excitement, fear, and doubt. I must have heard her wrong—Jax told me he was dead.

"My father—Elena, please tell me...is he alive?" My heart beats faster, anticipating her answer.

She grimaces. "It's so very complicated. I must talk quickly. Jax only gave me a small amount of time." She gazes into my eyes. "Your father is alive. No one knows where he is. When you were born, he took you away from your irrational mother to protect you. He kept you safe for a number of years, but he was tracked to Earth, so he fled before they could find you. He left you solely in my care. He chose me to protect you on Earth and keep you safe from Alala, your mother, the queen."

I barely recover from hearing "your father" and then she says "your mother." My hands start to visibly shake and the tears flow out of me like a waterfall. That doesn't stop

Elena from talking. She continues, though she puts her hand on mine, as she's done so many times before.

"I know this is difficult. I'm not sure what they'll tell you in here, so I'm trying to tell you everything. Your mother isn't a good woman. She once was, when your father first met her, but she changed. She's from Mapu, a neighboring planet. Your father met her many years ago when he worked for the military here on Pumalia. They quickly fell in love, and even though their union was frowned upon, they went against their families and were united.

"Mapu and Pumalia are rivals, and both of your parents had influential, powerful families. So their alliance sparked many issues between the two planets." Elena looks sad as she lifts her eyes to peer out the window.

"Elena, how did you know my father?" I can't believe this story and this woman sitting before me. She never breathed a word of this story—my story. And yet I'd been living in the same house with Elena for seventeen years— wait, it had to be less. Elena said I was a few years old when my father left me with her.

"Your father, Kalus, was in the military, as Jax is. Kalus fought for many years next to my father before my father was killed. After he died, I didn't have anyone, and your Kalus looked after me as if he were an older brother."

Elena must note the roil of emotions that have, no doubt, found their way to my face. She says in a pleading tone, "Alexa, I understand if you hate me for not telling you, but don't you see? I was doing everything I could to keep you safe."

Elena doesn't wait for a response before she digs into her jeans pocket and pulls out a folded yellow envelope. She slides out a key and a tiny map from the envelope and places them in my quivering hand. "When Jax comes for me, that will be your time to escape. Other than Maddox feeling threatened by your father, I don't know why they're keeping you locked up here. You're not dangerous. You're not evil. But you need to leave here as soon as possible. I've arranged transportation and someone to meet you outside the gates of the compound. You must sneak out of here. Use this map—it will lead you out through the back entrance.

"Jax isn't a bad person. He snuck me in here to see you, but he doesn't know I'm giving you this key," she says urgently. "As much as I want to trust him, always remember his sole alliance is to the Council and the people of Pumalia."

Just as Elena finishes, a knock sounds at the door. I panic and put my hands back on the edges of the bed to play the part of a restrained hostage. Elena jumps up and winks at me like she used to do before, when I would leave for school. This is her signal that everything will be okay. A flood of memories rushes into my mind, reminding me of our life together. With everything that's happened, it feels surreal and dreamlike.

She leans close one last time. "That must be my warning from Jax. I must go, Alexa. I love you. Take care of yourself. When you meet Kasper at the rear entrance, he will take you to a safe place. There, he will teach you about your abilities and why you're feared here at the compound. It's nothing to worry about.

"Wait ten minutes after I leave, then go. I'll create a diversion, and they'll be too busy to see you flee." She cradles my face in her hands and wipes my tears with her thumbs. This sounds like goodbye forever. "You must be brave, Alexa. Wait ten minutes and then go. I called in a favor and have arranged Gabby your nurse to be preoccupied, as well as have the door unguarded and the hall empty, but this will only last for a few minutes. That should allow you enough time to get away. Gabby is aware of the plan, as well, so don't expect her back. She's a kind being and knows that you should not be held here, this is a mistake."

"Thank you, Mom, for everything," I croak. I hope I can be as courageous as she thinks I'm. What if I fall asleep? I can't let her down. Nervously, I twirl my hair and bite my lip in an effort to stall my tears.

She nods. "Remember, you can do anything you put your mind to." She turns and rushes to the door. Just like that, she's gone. I may never see her again. That thought sends my residual tears into an uncontrollable sob. I bury my face in my hands. Only ten minutes to let go of Elena and the life I thought was mine.

I recite the words Elena said to me over and over again in my head: *"You can do anything."* I keep myself moving, thinking about all of the information she unloaded on me. I pace a few more times in front of the door, then push myself to open it. Trembling fear inches from my fingertips, through my body, all the way down to my toes.

I open the door a crack and peek through it into the corridor. To my surprise, there's no one there. This is my time—the time Elena risked herself to give me. I need to use this opportunity to escape.

I rock back and forth on my feet, half thinking I should stay and try to reason with these beings. I hate to think what might happen to my mom—I mean Elena—for helping me escape. My breathing rate steadily increases and my heart pounds. I need to make a decision, and quickly. I can hear ringing in my ears, and by now, I know that's a sign that I'm going to pass out. I try to calm myself with deep-breathing exercises and pleasant thoughts.

I picture Elena sacrificing her freedom—and possibly her life—to free me from this place. That's all I need to push me out the door. "One foot in front of the other," I whisper to myself. That becomes my chant to motivate myself to move.

I tiptoe to the end of the musty hall and peer left and right. Elena was right, no one in sight, the halls are empty. I glance down at the map in my hand. It indicates I should go right, so I do. I pick up my pace and jog to the next turn. I peer cautiously around the corner, but it's too dark to see anything. Fear freezes me in place. I just wish I could see down the hall! As I think that, a dim light turns on above my head. Briefly grateful, I decide to run.

The halls are lined with old portraits of men, possibly Council members, with their names and attributions to Pumalia. Part of me wants to stop and look for my father's picture, but I know I have to keep moving. It might not even be up there, anyway. Plus, I only have a limited amount of time and I must maximize it.

The stale smell grows stronger as I continue down the long hallway. The map indicates a door with stairs beyond it that descend to the basement. I know the door has to be here. Elena wouldn't lead me astray, but I can't see a door! I drag my hand along the cold cement wall, hoping I'll discover an inset doorknob or a concealed button that releases a hidden door. I can't find anything. Panic snakes along the back of my neck, but I make myself walk back a few steps and try again.

The second time around, I locate a slight depression in the wall, which is warmer than the rest of the concrete. This has to be the door on the map! I search for a doorknob or handle, but there's nothing.

I lean up against the door and push with all my strength. Did it move? If it did, it was so infinitesimal that it wasn't noticeable. I push again. Pause, and push again. After a few more attempts, the door begins to slowly creak open. A dark oblivion lies beyond the door. I pause and listen for movement, but I hear nothing, just my own blood whooshing through my ears. I shove the door open a tad more and squeeze myself through.

It's not only dark here, but the air is stagnant, as well. How long has it been since this passage was used? I ease the door back into place and start down the steps one at a time, moving slowly, inching my way with my feet on the steps and my hands groping for the wall.

Again, I think about Elena and her sacrifice. She's the only person I can truly trust, and I must do what she says, even though this—

The sound of running footsteps on the other side of the door startles me. The noise resembles a herd of charging elephants. The guards must know I'm no longer in my room. I have to pick up my pace before someone opens the door and finds me.

I know I'm approaching the bottom step because I can see a faint line of light under another door. That must be where I'm supposed to go. Relief washes over me— perhaps on the other side of this door is the way out of this prison.

Gathering all my strength, I lean into the heavy door. I'm able to hold it ajar long enough to slip outside. What I see shocks me. It's a courtyard populated with six uniformed men who seem to be guarding the very door that is supposed to symbolize my great escape!

After a moment's realization that I might actually be captured and taken back to my room, I duck behind a shrub and start to form a getaway plan. But when I peep through the bush and examine the courtyard, I also realize that my escape is probably not going to happen. The high walls are solid stone, smooth without any indentations or rock deformities that could provide foot or handholds, and though the uniformed men—men I've no hope of defeating—are spread out around the courtyard, they're blocking all exits.

I study the guard nearest me, determined to get by him. If only he would just disappear! I close my eyes to enjoy that fiction, imagining him dropping his weapon and simply disappearing. *I wish*, I think, opening my eyes again.

I blink in confusion. The guard is gone. I blink a few more times, but nothing changes. The only evidence that he was there is his firearm, lying near my feet only a few feet away from me. I shake my head in disbelief. How did that happen? Where did he go?

"Get her!" I hear one man yell to another.

I back up, but realize my capture is inevitable. *Nooo*, I groan mentally, tipping my head back and squeezing my eyes shut. If only I could soar above the compound and escape!

"Please don't hurt me," I call out, trying to reason with the guards. "I surrender."

Silence isn't the answer I expect for my plea.

I slowly open one eye. The guards are gone...and so am I. I feverishly blink my eyes. Where am I?

I'm hovering above the compound's stone wall.

I gaze down and watch two of the guards gawk at each other in disbelief. They run from the courtyard. They're probably going to get more guards to hunt me down. Quick, I need to think of something. I try not to shake but the trembles are unstoppable.

"No sudden moves, no sudden moves," I whisper, trying to focus on my breathing and on not falling— whatever that entails. I close my eyes and imagine myself safely back on the ground. My chant shifts to, "Please be on the ground, please be on the ground."

I flex my toes and they meet a surface. I open my eyes to find myself in the courtyard where the guards once were. Glancing down at the map, I identify the path that will lead me to Kasper, the person I'm supposed to meet. I step onto the path, relieved that it's bordered by tall hedges, concealing my passage. But when I reach the end, I realize this is where the map ends. I scan the perimeter and see no one.

I sigh. But Elena told me someone would be waiting.

My mind drifts back to the men disappearing and then me floating in midair. Really, this all feels more like a continuation of a dream than reality. If I'm not dreaming, and if it's not real, maybe I'm hallucinating?

Just as I begin to entertain the idea of dreaming and possibly being in my comfortable bed at home, I hear someone yell my name.

"Alexa! Over here—jump on. Hurry!"

I glance to my left and see some sort of two-wheeled, motorcycle-like contraption with a tall man driving it. If he thinks I'm riding that, he's crazy!

"Alexa, get on. The guards are coming."

I don't take any time to dwell on my decision. Despite my trepidation, I say a quick prayer and jump on. He knows my name, so I'm hoping this lanky man is Kasper.

Once we're out of there, he turns and says, "Hello, I'm Kasper."

Relief encompasses me and I'm finally able to breathe.

Until I think of Elena. Now I'm sick with worry for the only mother I've ever known.

Nine

THE JOURNEY TO WHEREVER we are going is taking more time than I anticipated. Surprisingly, the colorful landscape with its mountainous scenery keeps me occupied. The rolling hills meet each other with varying shades of green. Some hills are sprinkled with dense forests and some lie barren, creating a patchwork of greens. The looming trees are perfectly lined up and spaced equally apart, as if they were handpicked and placed there with a purpose. It instantly reminds me of my dreams. Scattered across the land are bodies of shimmering, cobalt water.

I keep looking behind me to make sure we aren't being followed, but no one appears to be there. In fact, I haven't seen any other being on this journey. The lengthy ride is peaceful, and I think if I weren't running from something, this scenic tour would be enjoyable. Oddly, this landscape reminds me of home. It isn't all that different than a ride up north, back on Earth. Instead of feeling millions of miles away from home, I'm reminded of driving to the University of Vermont last year, for a campus visit with my mom, Elena. I wonder if she ever thought that I would attend college, or was it wishful thinking on her part?

I notice that daylight is fading. I don't see a sun, but when I escaped, the sky was a bright pink. Now it's a darkening shade of violet. I hope that soon, we will be at our destination so I can finally ask some questions.

Part of me feels guilty for leaving that place without saying goodbye to Jax. I know he took me from my home, but he said he had no idea of Maddox's intentions, and I do believe him. I'm not sure why I believe him, but I do. Another part of me is angry at the fact that I believe a total stranger. I shake my head and try to focus on the task ahead—getting answers to my questions.

The motorcycle-like contraption starts to slow and we take a right down a narrow side road. It's more of a trail because the bush is overgrown, and we must duck as we navigate. Since the winding path requires a slower speed, Kasper lets up on the power and moves the vehicle skillfully around the trees and plants that obscure the way.

After weaving around plant life for a short time, we enter a clearing of glowing orange and red flowers that blossom from the mossy floor beneath us. We're literally in the middle of nowhere and it's growing darker by the minute. An uneasy queasiness travels through my stomach as we come to an abrupt halt. The dense forest surrounds us, and I worry we could be lost.

"Where are we?" I ask warily.

Kasper takes off his helmet and shakes out his black hair. It catches me by surprise, because his complexion is noticeably pale even with the dim light surrounding us. "So you are *the* Alexa Jenkinson?" His steel-gray eyes move over me from top to bottom.

"Yes, and you're Kasper?" I'm not sure why, but self-consciousness creeps along my body with the continued touch of his assessing gaze.

He awkwardly extends his hand and I shake it. It's warm and large wrapped around my small one. "Yes, that's me. I hope you don't normally jump on bikes with complete strangers." He snatches his hand free and spins back around to his bike. He shuts it down before glancing over his shoulder at me. "Let's go."

"Where are we going? How do you know Elena? Where are we?" My frustration level is growing.

"Whoa." He holds up a hand. "Let's take one thing at a time. Why don't we get to a safe place and then start discussing the answers?"

"Fine." I glance over at him just in time to see his smirk dissolve. I'm not sure why, but Kasper seems particularly odd to me. It's not just his contrasting skin and hair color, or his abnormally thin, tall body. It's his whole demeanor.

In an uncomfortable silence, we trek through the dimly lit woods. Thankfully the bioluminescent flowers provide a trail beneath my feet. The trees are the tallest I've ever seen. Even the water is glowing. Clean and clear, it shimmers brightly without sunlight. We're walking too fast for me to see if there are any creatures that live in the water, but I imagine they're there. Every once in a while, out of the corner of my eye, I see something create a ripple on the water's surface.

Before too long, I realize that the sky is darkening to a coffee-brown color. Night is here. Kasper starts walking faster and to catch up I must jog. His legs are a lot longer than mine, so it's easy for me to fall behind.

Just as I catch up to him, he stops. "We're here." His voice startles me. I haven't heard it in some time.

"Where exactly is 'here'?" I turn a complete circle, searching for a sign of a structure that we can take shelter in, but there's nothing.

"You'll see." His smirk returns, and I can tell he is having fun with me. He loves seeing me impatient and waiting for the next bit of information.

He saunters over to a tall tree that has a purple-tinged trunk contrasting with its luscious, green leaves. With his index finger, he draws a design or some sort of symbol on the bark. I stand there thinking this guy is a tad crazy. However, before I can finish the thought, the ground below us vibrates. I close my eyes in trepidation; we'll either be swallowed up by the forest floor, or squished by a falling tree, I'm sure of it.

The trembling finally stops and I open my eyes. Right before my feet, a stairway descends into the ground beneath us.

"Well, what're you waiting for, Alexa?" He's standing on the first step, waving for me to proceed in front of him.

"It's dark down there. Can't you go first?" Embarrassed by my hesitation, I duck my head, hiding my face behind my now very frizzy hair.

"I need to shut the door behind us. It's necessary I'm last. Ms. Jenkinson, if you're afraid..." He hurriedly waves me forward like he's exasperated that I'm taking too much time to advance past him.

"No, I'm not afraid. I just don't know where I'm going," I say, but honestly, I'm a little frightened. I don't want him to think I'm a wimp, so I put one foot in front of the other and proceed down the pitch-black steps.

After everything that's happened to me, I have to say I didn't expect to be surprised. But I step off the last step and gaze around, dumbstruck. A subterranean city sprawls in front of me. Its sheer grandness takes my breath away. I wouldn't have imagined a place like this could exist underground. Buildings stretch into the distance, and people are walking around.

"W-what's this place?" I manage, trying not to stare.

"This is where we displaced Aliens live. 'We' being the breeds that no longer can live freely on our own planets, due to the hostility and war brought about by your family." He steps in front of me to lead the way.

"I'm sorry this has happened." I can't help but feel guilty from his last statement. I had no idea that my "family" even existed before all of this craziness. Yet even though I've nothing to do with the turmoil he speaks of, I can't help thinking I'm somewhat responsible.

We walk down a cobblestone path toward the outskirts of this mysterious city. Floral scents tickle my nose and I struggle to hold back a sneeze. The buildings are as tall as the trees I saw while walking in the forest. I also see small structures with food in the windows—probably stores. Sectioned-off fields that appear before me resemble a large garden. Streams bisect the garden and beings are bustling along the cobblestone paths. Soft murmurs surround us. I'm unable to make out the faint voices and what's being said, but I can tell there are many conversations happening at once.

My mouth hangs open in amazement, not only that this place exists, but that it's completely underground—even the garden! There are no moons or stars, just artificial light. "What is this place called?"

"Aurora, after the Roman goddess of dawn, because this place is always in the light, even if it's a lowlight," Kasper answers. "You'll see aliens here from all around the galaxy. They may appear different, especially with the varying glow, but please don't stare at them. They could get angry and attack you if you do, so just keep walking. This is the main reason why we keep this place almost perpetually illuminated. The dark brings out the beings' true planetary forms, and it can be intimidating, especially for new aliens."

"Are you calling me a new alien? Am I an alien?" I squeal.

"Well, yes, you're not from Aurora, so you are," he says. He gestures toward the city. "Here, residents are referred to as either a being or an alien. Anything other than those two words could upset them, so please, no matter who you talk to, don't insult them." His voice turns hard, making that an order.

"Beings, aliens, true planetary forms...attacks!" I grumble. "What else can you possibly surprise me with?"

"Oh, Alexa, you have so much to learn," he sighs. "Let's get settled and start doing that—it may be a lengthy process."

"Okay, but why are you helping me?"

Kasper grins, clearly entertained by my straightforward question. "I'm doing this for Elena. Before she became your guardian, she was instrumental in creating Aurora. She worked with us day in and day out to create a safe place where we would not be found." He draws a deep breath and releases it slowly. "Her father also helped us create new lives for ourselves, and he helped transport us here unseen. I owe Elena and her family a lot. I would do anything she asked of me."

Kasper turns down a path to the right and approaches a wooden door. He presses his palm against the door, and a few moments later, it opens. "This is my home," he says to me.

We enter a living space equipped with a sink, a sitting area, and a bed in the corner. The place is small, but neat, so tidy that it appears as if no one actually lives here. The walls are plain white and devoid of any decoration or personal belongings. The bed is much longer than the one I have at home—to accommodate Kasper's tall frame, no doubt. There are no appliances in the area near the sink, just a basket holding oddly shaped fruit in unfamiliar colors.

"There is a place to tidy up in the corner. Would you like to shower and freshen up? It's nothing like you're accustomed to, but it's something." He waves toward the washroom and starts to walk away, but he abruptly turns around. "I also have a change of clothes for you in there."

I perk up at the thought of washing the grime of that dungeon off of me. "Thank you, I really appreciate it."

"I will also prepare you something to eat."

Without hesitation, I move toward the washroom. "Thank you, Kasper," I say as I enter and close the door. The room is tiny and dark, but I welcome the chance to shower and have a few minutes to myself to reflect on the craziness that's transpired.

A large part of me still fears what Elena's fate was for freeing me. Did she get caught? Is she okay? I'm not even sure if I'll ever know and that alone churns my stomach.

Strangely, I still feel bad for leaving Jax. I know I shouldn't, but there's no denying that I feel oddly connected to him. I also believe that he truly had no idea what was going to happen to me. He seemed genuinely stunned at Maddox's request.

Opening the slender shower door, I find to my surprise a tall, narrow shower stall hewn right into the rock of the great underground cavern's walls. The dark material makes the small stall seem murky, but it's shiny, which helps. I squeeze myself inside and let the water cleanse my grimy body. Maybe if I close my eyes tight enough, I can imagine being back at home on Earth, going about my life.

I picture myself getting ready for school—better yet, getting ready for my walk to school with Michael. It's the Monday after the dance and we are reminiscing about how much fun we had and making plans for the following weekend. I slowly open my eyes and see the black, slate shower walls staring back at me. I quickly finish and step out onto the bathroom floor, which is also that strange dark slate. I grab the towel hanging on the wall and wrap myself tight.

The sound of voices slink under the door and I strain to hear what's being said. There's no mistaking one of the hushed tones as Kasper's. The other voice is a woman's. I can't tell what they're saying, but I know whatever it is, they don't want me to hear.

I dry myself briskly off and get dressed. It's weird that Kasper has a prepared change of clothes for me. The black pants are a little short, but they will do. However, the pink tank top fits perfectly. I hang my towel back on the wall and hurry out to see who is here.

I was expecting someone similar to Kasper; instead, it's a girl a little shorter than me. She appears to be about my age, with black hair cascading halfway down her back. When she turns around, she catches me off guard. She's very pale, sparkly skin and large, piercing purple eyes. Something about her is very attractive. I wonder if she's Kasper's girlfriend.

She takes two steps toward me, her smile forced. "You must be Alexa."

"Um, yeah," I mutter awkwardly.

"I'm Tam. I've been awaiting your arrival. I hope the clothes fit." She scans me up and down. "They'll do for now."

"Yes, they fit. Thank you." I'm not sure what else to say to her. I still have so many questions, but would she be able to answer them?

"I'm sorry, I have to run out again. There's a lot to do, now that you're here. We must get to work. Plus, it's getting dark, and I don't want you to feel uncomfortable." She opens the door and dashes out, not even giving me time to respond to her odd comment.

"Do you feel better, Alexa?" Kasper asks.

"Yes, I guess so. I'm still so confused. Why does she think she'll make me uncomfortable?" I say in a near-whisper.

His expression mildly perplexed, Kasper leans against the wall and studies me as if I'm some sort of science experiment. His staring is so intense, I peer down at the floor and take a deep breath, hoping that will generate a response of some sort. What's he thinking?

I finally break down. "What?"

Quickly, his gaze turns playful and a knowing grin inches across his face.

"Am I amusing you?" I snap.

He finally nods enthusiastically and comments, "There's just so much to tell you. And since it's getting darker, I'm watching your true form start to show. It is indeed amusing."

"What do you mean, my true form?" Bile wriggles up the back of my throat. My body is warm, feverish. What does he see?

"Well, Alexa, since you're half Pumalian and half Mapu, your true form will depend on what planet you're on. When nighttime comes, or in Aurora's case, when the artificial light dims into darkness, all beings appear in their true forms—although not to their fullest extent. What you saw earlier on our walk here is the acceptable alien form for traveling—it won't alarm humans or other aliens. It's almost like camouflage.

"Since we all have to live together here, it's best to have the option of both. Some aliens can really be uptight around the beings whose true forms include multiple heads and towering stature."

I can tell he's enjoying my squirming discomfort. "You're joking, right?" I drop my gaze to my hands, breaking our eye contact.

He draws a deep breath and says, "You won't look too different than you do now. Just a few subtle changes, like hair color, eye color, and perhaps skin color and height. But don't worry. These changes will be in effect only in darkness. During the day, when there's sunlight, you'll appear in the same likeness as you did on Earth. Eventually, once you're on your home planet for a long enough period of time, either here on Pumalia or Mapu, you'll change less and less in the dark. We're on Pumalia, but underground, so the effects are lessened at this depth."

"What? You think those are a few things? What's left?" My lungs tighten, the early stages of dizziness tease my conscience, and hyperventilation is inevitable. I don't want him to see that I'm upset, but at the same time, he just told me my true form is beginning to show. How could this be? I don't feel any different. I inspect my hands again. My skin seems shinier.

Kasper adds, "For example, Tam—she's from Pumalia, and her features are stronger down here than most. Dark hair and purple eyes are a common characteristic for Pumalia and Mapu."

"I'll have purple eyes?" I cry.

"There's a mirror in the closet if you want to see for yourself." His voice drips with enjoyment.

I shake my head. "I'm all set. I think I'm going to sleep. I'm very tired and I have a lot to process." I walk over to the couch and plop myself down. I really don't want to talk to him any longer. He makes me nervous, and I think he knows it. Even more, I think he likes it.

"Whatever you want, Alexa. I'm actually going to step out for a bit—I don't want my true form to scare you on the first night. Make yourself at home. I'll be back by the time you wake up."

I watch him gather a few things and leave. I'm all by myself on another planet, underground. All of this is so surreal. I close my eyes and try to remember my once-boring life.

The orange light creeping through the windows startles me awake. I open my eyes and realize that I'm still on Kasper's couch and not where I want to be: in my comfortable bed back on Earth.

I peer over the back of the couch to see Kasper and Tam sitting quietly. Tam looks appalled, Kasper somewhat relieved.

I swallow my uneasiness, rise, and approach them. "Are you guys waiting for me?"

"Is she kidding?" Tam mutters under her breath.

"Sort of," Kasper answers nonchalantly. "We need to start informing you of what's happening."

"Why didn't you wake me up?" I fire back, annoyed. Why were they just waiting for me?

Suddenly defensive, Tam jumps to her feet. "We did, and you threw the chair at me!"

Tam's outburst makes me laugh out loud. She has to be crazy. I can't lift and throw chairs, especially when sleeping.

I turn to her companion. "Kasper, I'm not sure why Elena wanted me to come with you, but I'm ready to leave. I don't need to be yelled at by an Alien!"

Tam shoots Kasper a look of disproval and sits back down.

"Alexa, I told you there are things we need to go over, and the sooner, the better. Tam is just upset because you attempted to kill her." Kasper's voice is so calm that I can't possibly believe what he's saying. How can someone act so calm and tell lies like this?

"I didn't try to kill her. I was sleeping on the couch. Are you both crazy?" I start to pace angrily in front of them.

"Relax, Alexa, we know you didn't do it on purpose. But that's why we need to start briefing you on your potential abilities."

Kasper's know-it-all attitude only frustrates me more. The anger sinks into the pit of my stomach and releases a tingling sensation into my body. My arms begin to shake and my fingers start to glow.

"Alexa, listen to me." His tone is suddenly urgent. "Take a deep breath and calm down before you do something we'll all regret."

"What's happening to me?" I stare down at my hands in disbelief. Ten tiny glowing flashlights illuminate the ends of my fingers. The room begins to spin. I close my eyes and concentrate on what Kasper said. I take a few deep breaths.

"This is just great," Tam whispers.

"Tam, you're not helping here. Please, hush," Kasper hisses.

I open my eyes. The spinning room comes to a screeching halt. I see my ten fingers are no longer glowing, and Kasper and Tam are watching me in wide-eyed disbelief.

"Apparently, you two have a lot to tell me." Embarrassment heats my face. I keep my eyes on the table, trying to avoid the awkward situation.

"The thing is, Alexa, we don't have all of the answers. We don't know exactly what your powers are—that is, besides throwing chairs in your sleep and your fingers lighting up. We can assume that telekinesis is among your skills, but that's all we can assume. It could be a lot more." Kasper's expression is serious, his smirk gone.

I nod. "When do we begin?"

"Now," they say in unison.

I pull a chair out and sit down across from them.

Ten

I WOULD BE LYING if I said the past two days were lacking answers. In all reality, the past two days have made me question my sanity and basically everything else I've ever known.

Kasper and Tam are turning out to be pretty cool aliens. Sometimes I pretend I'm in New York City, because this underground planet is a giant melting pot for extraterrestrials that are having problems on their own planet. I've been too tired to stay up to see their true forms—or mine, for that matter. I want to take that part of the process very slowly because honestly, I'm really freaked out.

Tam filled me in on my mother. She told me that she's a power monger on the planet Mapu and is known all over the galaxy for her tyrannical ways. Apparently, she was born into a Mapu family that held a spot in the oligarchy, but over the years, the numbers of powerful families have dwindled, so now it's solely her running the planet. She refers to herself as the queen and no one challenges her.

Then there's the story of my father, because a crazy mother isn't enough. He was born on Pumalia and his mother was also Pumalian, but his father was from a distant, now extinct planet, Plito. My grandfather had significant powers that were passed down to my father. Those powers are what make my fingers light up, send electrical currents through my body, and allow me to throw things without picking them up; it's possible they aided me in my escape from the castle, too.

Kasper thinks my father had a master plan that included hiding me on Earth with Elena as my pseudo-mother. They assume that he hid me so my lovely mother wouldn't use my powers against her enemies. I have yet to confirm if my powers are really all that powerful. Right now, I'm learning what provokes them, and I haven't had much luck controlling them. Unfortunately, I don't have any brothers or sisters to ask, and my parents are not resources I can go to either, so I'm left here trying to figure it all out.

Kasper and Tam also seem to think that, based on some of my grandfather's other abilities, besides telekinesis, my powers could include some form of mind control and, possibly, time travel. They know someone who can help me explore these abilities, but I want a few more days to learn about my history and the general history of the galaxy before I'm all mighty and powerful. That sounds like a joke, but I guess we will have to wait and see.

Also, Kasper has heard that in the time we've been hiding here, there has been a full-scale search driven by Maddox and his people to find me. I can't help but wonder if Jax is searching for me as well.

"Kasper," I announce suddenly, "I'm going for a walk." He looks up from his book and silently nods. These four walls taunt me, I must escape and breathe.

"Don't be long; we have much more to discuss, and Tam will be back soon. You know how she hates waiting," he adds.

I roll my eyes in his direction and march out of the house. The temperature here seems to vary, which strikes me as odd. We're underground; the air would normally be stale and warm, but it isn't.

I stroll down the cobblestone path and pass by the center of town. Not too many beings are out and about. I can't say I blame them, since it will soon be dark. That's why I want to get out for some air and alone time before the twilight settles in.

Every time I venture from the house, I find myself drawn to the edge of town. I like to sit on the rocks and pretend that this really isn't happening to me. I watch a beautiful, natural, cascading waterfall and it soothes my nerves.

I close my eyes and try to remember the dreams I had prior to my arrival. Jax was so warm and comforting. I truly believed I was safe with him. Something about him was familiar.

Curling up on the rock, I relive my last moments with Jax. He was in my room, watching me. Why would he have done that if he were trying to capture me from the beginning?

"Alexa, where are you?"

Jax's voice. I can hear it, but how?

"Jax?" Am I imagining his voice? I blink and open my eyes. My only comfort is the cool breeze from the waterfall. I close my eyes again. I hear his voice.

"Alexa, I'm looking for you. I want to help you. You're in danger. Tell me where you are—I'll come and get you." I can tell by his voice that he's sincere.

"I'm okay, Jax, don't worry about me." Part of me wants to tell him everything. I want him to come and get me. "How are we talking?"

"I'm not sure, but for some reason I can hear you in my head. It feels like you're looking for me. I can't explain it."

His voice wavers with uncertainty, but I know that maybe this is one of my powers.

"It's safe here. I'm learning about who I am." I try to sound confident, but part of me wonders who I can really trust. That reminds me that I have to go before it gets dark.

"Alexa, be careful. From what I've learned about you and your family, it will be hard to trust anyone. You come from an elite bloodline, and you possess the ability to be a real game-changer."

"Thank you for telling me, but I must go." I sweep my gaze over the familiar surroundings—the waterfall, the city in the distance. It's getting darker. That realization scares me enough to jump to my feet. In my mind, I try to send Jax a message not to worry about me. But who knows if he'll even get it.

I collect my thoughts and slowly descend from my perch. When I land on the ground, I know I'm not alone. I try to keep my composure and look around without being too obvious.

One foot in front of the other, I keep repeating in my head. Even though I keep moving forward, I know that the being is closing in on me. I decide to take a stand. I spin around to confront my stalker, but no one is there.

"I know you're there," I say, my voice riddled with worry.

The path behind me has tall green shrubs on both sides. It's a place where anyone could hide, I realize, and fear paralyzes me as I wait. A few moments pass.

Then he steps out of a patch of greenery.

"Alexa, I'm sorry, I didn't mean to scare you."

"Michael! What are you doing here?" My eyes must be deceiving me. My heart starts to beat harder and faster. I'm staring at the boy I left on Earth, in my old life.

"Well, I thought you would be happier to see me," he jokes.

I shake my head in disbelief. He grabs my hand and pulls me closer. His dark-brown eyes shimmer in the twilight, sending a trail of goosebumps down my arm.

Forcing myself to step back, I stand there trying to absorb what I'm actually seeing. "But how could you be here?" My voice shudders with surprise.

"Looks like I'm not the only one who has been keeping secrets." He flashes me his beautiful smile and I can feel myself slowly melting inside.

"Michael, what are you doing here? How did you get here?" His gaze hasn't left my face while I anxiously await his answers.

"Alexa, sit down and I'll explain everything."

I stumble backward and perch myself on a rock. I feel nauseous, overloaded by trying to process everything.

"Are you okay?" I can tell by the tone of his voice that he's sympathetic to how I'm dealing with another new development in this crazy nightmare. "Honestly, I didn't mean to scare you. It's just important that no one else sees me."

"Why, who are you? How did you get here?" I demand. My chest tightens. Tears will be next. I'm physically and mentally exhausted.

"Alexa, how much do you know about yourself? Like where you really come from?" He leans against the nearest tree and stares at me, waiting for an answer.

"All I know for sure is that this is messed up and I want to go home." And in that instant, the tears start pouring out of me. I'm embarrassed, but only for a minute.

Michael takes my hands and tugs me down off the rock. "Please, don't cry." He wipes the tears from my face and draws me against him. His familiar, sweet, musky scent instantly comforts me. I let him hold me until he pries me off, distancing himself from me. "I'll explain."

"Please do, because a few days ago we were taking a Biology exam and now we are on a different Planet in some underground alien hideout. So please tell me who you are and why you're here." My last request sounds more like a plea than a question.

"I'm like you, Alexa. I'm not from Earth. I was born and raised on Mapu. I'm not here to upset you. I've come for you."

"I'm sorry, Michael. This is just all so hard. So much has happened. My mom isn't really my mom and she might be dead because of me..."

His eyebrows furrow and I can tell he's debating whether he should tell me something. He opens his mouth, but no words came out at first. Then he says, "Alexa, I'll tell you everything, but right now, I need you to listen to me." Gazing up at the artificial sky, then back down to me, he warns, "We don't have much time. Our true forms will be appearing soon, and I don't want you to be scared or alarmed."

"So you're just like me? I mean we both are *really* aliens from somewhere other than Earth." The possibility of this being true alleviates some tension. I'm not alone.

I draw away, wondering if my transformation is already in process. My face is warming. What if my transformation scares him off? "What're we going to do?" I ask.

He takes in his surroundings, his gaze distant while he thinks, mentally forming a plan. "We could go through it together. Or we could meet up in a few hours, when the light gets brighter." I can tell the last option isn't his first preference.

"Do you know what your features are in alien form?" I don't mean for the words to sound so harsh, but I can't help wondering how bad it could really be.

Michael levels a stare at me with his eyebrows raised. "Yes, I do. You don't?"

"No." I bite my lip out of frustration and cross my arms over my chest. I probably appear to be throwing a tantrum, but I'm just upset at myself for not having the courage to look the first night.

"We can do it together, then. I've an idea, because of your background, what you might resemble. Don't be nervous; you'll be beautiful, just as you are right now." He lifts my chin with his thumb so I'm staring him in the eyes. "Trust me, Alexa. It won't be awful." He reassures me with a grin and a wink.

"Okay, but first, what should I expect to see from you?" Nerves make me start to tremble. Not knowing what to envision is dreadful. Michael is so cute, and the idea of him turning into an alien is ridiculous.

Petrifying.

"Ah, you're nervous I'll be scary?" He tries unsuccessfully to hide his grin, but the dimples indenting his cheeks give it away.

And that's when it hits me. Why do I care what my alien form is? This is who I am and I need to accept that. It can't be that bad if Michael is willing to reveal his identity and see mine.

"No. I'm okay. Let's do it." I study the light above. It's nearly faded completely, and even if I want to change my mind, it's too late.

"Close your eyes," Michael says. "I'll tell you when it's over. It should only take a few minutes." He grabs my hands and squeezes them to reassure me.

The anticipation is the worst. I keep imagining Michael with a large head, big eyes, and a long, green body. Sweat beads on my forehead and I wonder if I'll be green with additional appendages.

It seems an eternity passes, but it has really only been a few minutes before Michael says, "Alexa, you're gorgeous." I can feel Michael's gaze upon me. "You're pretty much the same. I'm afraid you're a little bit shorter, but you appear stronger. Your muscles are well-defined and, not to be rude, but you're curvier." He gives my hands another squeeze, signaling that it's okay to open my eyes.

I blink a few times to accustom my sight to the dark. Michael's face is no longer directly across from mine. I'll have to crook my neck to see his face. Either he grew, or I shrank considerably.

I slowly lift my gaze and my eyes meet his. He still resembles Michael, but he's taller, his Beiber hair is longer and a lot darker, and his eyes are the color of steel. He's absolutely captivating.

"Are you okay?" His voice is the same, and I can sense his concern.

"Huh? Yeah, I'm okay. You just—you're so...so different." I stare at him in awe. He smiles. I think he knows what I'm trying to say. He's hot. Popular Earth Michael is actually a hot, model alien. This is crazy.

"The clothes are a tad tight, but I came to you as quickly as I could, and I didn't grab anything to change into." Now that he mentions it, his shirt *is* on the verge of ripping. His biceps bulge within his sleeves, and I can see the outline of the muscles on his chest and stomach.

Nervously, I stare down at my body to make sure I'm still fully clothed. My pants fit me fine. Stretchy leggings, thankfully, so they're easily adjustable. However, my tank top is now a tad too small. My chest definitely grew a size. Now I know what Michael meant when he said "curvier."

"Do you want to see how beautiful you are?" he asks.

Mentally, I'm not sure if I can handle all of these changes, but after seeing Michael's unscary change, I decide I should. "Yes, I think I'm ready."

He leads me by the hand back to the boulder where I fell asleep, and easily lifts me up onto it. I kneel down and glance at my reflection in the stream. The light is dim so I know I can't see myself perfectly, and before I can think twice about the darkness my fingertips light up. Since this isn't the first time I don't freak out but instead immediately worry how Michael will take the news.

"Um, so yeah my fingertips glow or ignite and I have no control." Instantly I blush and hope he isn't repulsed by the new Alien me.

"Wow! I've heard of this phenomenon but I've never seen it, never mind up close." He quickly moves his eyes from the tips of my fingers to my face. His look of shock is quickly replaced by a devious grin.

I use my fingers as a light source and peer back into the water prepared to be disgusted by my new look, but what I see is surprising. My facial features are pretty much the same, except now I have high cheekbones. My eyes are larger, more oval, and definitely a darker color, a beautiful deep lavender. My hair is longer and strikingly dark against my pale, almost translucent skin. I'm not scary; I'm stunning.

"What do you think?" Michael asks eagerly.

"I'm, uh...pretty." I try to hide my shock, but my quavering voice gives me away. I sit back on my heels and lock my stare with his.

"You've always been beautiful, Alexa." Smiling, Michael gazes into my eyes.

"Thanks, Michael, but don't think a compliment like that's going to get you out of doing some pretty intense explaining," I half joke. He drops his eyes and his posture stiffens. I twist around to sit on the rock facing him. "Who are you? How did you find me?"

Michael glances up. His gray eyes are darker, and I can almost feel his tension radiating between us. "I don't know how to explain all of this. I never wanted to lie to you. I'll tell you what I can."

All I want is answers, but I can see by Michael's expression that the answers aren't good.

"Before I moved to Massachusetts, I was living on the planet Mapu. That's where I'm from. My job was to go to Earth and get to know you."

His words hit me like a slap in the face. My mother must have sent him. "Do you know she wants to kill me?"

Michael jumps off the rock and puts his hands on my waist to pull me down with him. "I would never let anyone hurt you, Alexa," he says earnestly. "You didn't let me finish." I try to break free, but his strength is insurmountable. He holds me gently but tightly until I stop fighting him.

"Why did you pretend to like me and ask me to the dance?" I say as humiliation spreads like poison through my body. I'm simply a job. Anger quickly replaces the embarrassment.

"Alexa, please calm down. You're not a job. I really wanted to go to the dance with you." Michael looks uneasily at me and I realize my fingers are still glowing but the color has deepened from sun kissed orange to a blood red. I close my eyes and take a few deep breaths, hoping that will cure my weirdness.

"You can open your eyes."

My knees buckle. Michael catches me and keeps his arms around me to hold me upright. A long moment passes before I notice that he's smiling and my fingers are no longer glowing. "What's so funny?" I pull away from him and fold my arms across my chest.

Great, so now he's making fun of my alien oddness.

"I'm not laughing *at* you. I'm smiling because even now, here on this planet, you're so sensitive. I thought it was an insecure Earth thing, but you're just emotional." He pulls his smile into a sly smirk and glances to the side, avoiding my death stare.

"Great. So not only was I a job to you, I was too sensitive." I know he doesn't mean to hurt me with his comments, but it's frustrating when people think they know who I am better than I do.

"That's not what I mean, Alexa. But I'm sorry if I hurt you. Can you forgive me?" He puckers his face and sticks out his bottom lip in a perfect pout.

I can't help but grin at his playfulness. "I'm not sure if I do, but I'll think about it."

"Good, that's all I can ask. Now that we've transitioned, let me answer any questions that you have." He grabs my hand and leads me a few steps into the dense shrubs beside the waterfall.

Moments later, we come upon two sleeping bags, a campfire, and a thermos. I turn and gaze back the way we came. There's a nearly unobstructed view of the waterfall. "Michael, were you here while I was on the rock by the river napping?" Where I was while dreaming and talking with Jax, my mind adds.

"Yes, I was keeping an eye on you. I'd just found you, and I wasn't going to let you out of my sight." Michael crouches to stir the fire to life. Then he pats the nearest sleeping bag, inviting me to sit next to him. He opens the thermos and takes a few swallows, then passes it my way. I take it hesitantly and he chuckles. "Don't worry, it's not poison."

I roll my eyes and take a swallow. It tastes sweeter than any water I've tasted before. "What's this?" I take another swallow and savor the taste.

"It's water from the river you were sitting next to. It's the purest water around." He rolls his neck, then gazes directly into my eyes. It almost feels like we're back in my bedroom, prepping for the biology test. Until I scan him from head to toe and take in his new muscular appearance.

"Michael, why are you here?" I whisper, staring into his eyes.

"I'm here for you. There are a lot of people searching for you, and I'm going to take you to a safe place. Do you know who you truly are? What you're capable of?" His voice is now serious, which concerns me.

"Well, I was told that my father is some type of military warrior who was thought to be dead but actually isn't. And my mom is some evil matriarch on the planet Mapu. Is this right?"

"Pretty much." Michael's voice is low.

"Great," I mutter sarcastically. But I can sense he isn't telling me everything. He's holding back and that makes me nervous.

"Do you know what your powers are?" He bites his bottom lip and holds his breath, waiting for my answer.

"Not quite. Kasper told me there's no way to know the extent until I produce some sort of new skill. I know I've extra strength and I can light up a room with my hands when I get angry. I also know sometimes when I imagine something or think about something, I can make it happen. But that's only happened once or twice." I study my folded hands.

"Hmmm, there are a lot of things you might be capable of. Therefore, there are quite a few people who would like to get a hold of you."

"But why, Michael? I don't understand why they want me. I don't even know how to use my possible powers." I truly can't believe I'm a target because of something I *might* be able to do.

"Alexa, there's an intergalactic war happening right now. Planets are fighting for resources to stay alive. This panics the aliens and they flee their planets, seeking a safer, more habitable place. This whole underground city was created to hide aliens that have already left their planets." Michael's voice quivers with the last word, indicating how serious this situation is.

"I know that's what I was told. It just seems like something out of a movie. Even hearing it from you, it sounds unbelievable. I just don't know why aliens can't come and go when they want. Especially if their own planet is in such turmoil."

"There are rules in the galaxy to prevent that. You're supposed to stay on the planet you were born to, even if it's dying. If you flee, then you're punished," he replies.

"That's stupid! Who made that rule?" I can't believe that there are aliens stuck on a dying planet.

"Your mother," he almost groans.

"But why would she care?" It baffles me that one being holds so much authority.

"She wants to hold all power over the galaxy. Other planets cower at her demands because they're afraid of her cruelty. She tortures and kills aliens for all sorts of insignificant reasons." Michael looks down, and I can tell by his expression that his mind is somewhere else.

"Why does she want me?" I ask, fearing the answer.

"You're believed to have the abilities to help her rule the galaxy. Others believe you have the ability to stop her and save the galaxy from its demise."

"No!" I yell, jumping to my feet. "I need to go. I need to go back home. This is too much. I can't be here."

Michael hops up and grabs me by the arm. "It's not who you are, Alexa. I know that, and soon, more will know what I know. You're good, nothing like her." He puts his hands on my hips and draws me in to him once again, comforting me. "You're so special." His lips are inching closer to mine. I lift my chin, closing the gap between us. His lips are so full and warm against mine. They part and his tongue tickles my bottom lip.

Our first kiss. I pull back, unable to comprehend what's happening. His eyes travel up and down my body. His shoulders fall as he lets out a deep breath. He moves in again and takes my face in his hands. He stares passionately into my eyes and moves closer. I close my eyes, longing for another kiss. His lips graze mine and I let out a low moan.

Michael moves his lips down my neck. I pull away, afraid that all of this excitement will trigger a magical reaction.

"I'm sorry, Alexa," he says. "I've been wanting to do that since we studied in your bedroom."

"That's okay." I can't keep my lungs full enough with sweet air. "What do we do next? What do I tell Kasper and Tam?"

"Nothing. We must leave without them knowing. If we tell them where we're going, they could also be in danger."

"Where will we go, then?" I really can't imagine putting more people in danger because of who I am.

"We will go where they least expect. For now, we rest for a few hours. Then we'll leave." He sits back down on the sleeping bag and I follow his lead. "By the way, happy birthday, Alexa."

"Thank you." I look away, afraid that I might tear up again. He pulls his sleeping bag closer and lies behind me with his arm draped around me. It makes me feel safe and not alone. His nose tickles my neck as I curl up against him. He kisses the top of my head so gently, like he's afraid I'll break. For that moment, I pretend to be back at home with Michael, enjoying the dance. It's the last thing I think of before sleep finds me.

"Alexa...

I can hear Michael's voice faintly in my head, but I find it difficult to open my eyes. "Okay, I'm getting up," I reply dreamily. I blink my eyes a few times, then take in my surroundings.

Michael is standing above me with a wide smile on his face. "Wow, waking you up is a difficult job. I've been trying for at least twenty minutes." He offers his hand to help me to my feet, then pulls me close and bends his head down to whisper in my ear, "Are you ready to be on the run with me?" His warm breath shoots tingles through my body, and a weakness sweeps through me making my legs wobble. I'm thankful he's holding me up, otherwise, I'm not sure I'd be standing.

He tips my face up and kisses me with mind-boggling tenderness. I wasn't expecting it, but I don't stop him, either. Instead, I kiss him back, and the moment turns from tender into a feverish whirlwind. His hands are traveling over my body, leaving my skin hot wherever they touch. I run my fingers through his soft, dark hair and down his muscle-etched back. He moves his mouth from my lips to my neck. My stomach swirls with both anticipation and nervousness. I bring my hands to his chest and push him back.

His steel-gray eyes flutter open. They appear even lighter, touched with a swirl of blue. The corners of his mouth tip upward in a grin. "I could get used to that," he comments.

He bends down and starts to pick up our supplies. I decide to help him instead of standing and watching him. I try to make the silence more bearable by pelting him with questions about where we're going. The only answer he reveals is something about it being the best, least obvious place to hide out. I decide to let the topic rest for now.

I can't stop feeling bad about leaving Kasper and Tam. They really seemed dedicated to helping me learn how to use my powers. But if what Michael says is true, I'd better stick with him. I just hope Kasper understands that if I stay, I put everyone down here in danger. The gravity of the overall situation really weighs on me. How could I let this queen—my mother—scare or even kill these poor beings?

"Alexa, stop worrying. We'll find a way to get you out of this mess." Michael flashes me a quick smile while putting the last of the supplies in his backpack.

"It's not that, Michael. I just wish my mother wasn't a monster terrorizing all these beings. There has to be something I can do to stop her."

"It's not that easy, but we will come up with something," he replies.

"Where are we going now?" Where could we be going to stay safe? "Aren't we in a good place to hide out?"

"No. There are beings down here that have seen you. They would use your whereabouts to save themselves by striking a deal with the queen. We can't take that chance." Michael holds my gaze. He doesn't have to speak more; his stern demeanor says it all. He grabs my hand and slings the backpack over his shoulder.

I notice Michael's hair is becoming lighter and the steeliness in his eyes is receding. However, his muscular physique remains. I give my body a downward sweeping glance. My hair is lighter too, although it's still longer than it was on Earth.

"Michael, the lighting is getting stronger, but parts of you still appear different. Why is that?" I try not to sound surprised, but just when I think I understand what's happening, something changes.

Michael stops and turns toward me. He studies my face as he speaks. "Alexa, the more time you spend on your planet or near it, the more you show your heritage. After a few days, there will be subtle changes to your appearance—unless you leave and go somewhere else that's not your place of origin. It's almost like a disguise. We all possess this ability to hide our true appearance so we're not targeted by a rival planet."

"So, our true form is always visible when we're on the planet we belong to?"

"Yes, it's like a protective barrier between you and strangers. I may still appear different because here on Pumalia, I'm closer to Mapu than I was on Earth." Michael reaches up and brushes the hair out of my face. "You're so beautiful, Alexa."

That's all it takes to twist my stomach with anticipation. His touch is so soft and caring. He lowers his lips to mine and gently kisses me, taking my mind off whatever we were just talking about. I tangle my hand in his thick hair and let myself live in the moment. He lifts me up so he doesn't have to bend over. He guides my legs to wrap around him, freeing his hands to wander over my body.

Only moments later, he pulls back and sets me on the ground again. Lack of air, or change of mind? When I gaze up at him, I notice his eyes filling up. I decide not to ask him why he stopped, and follow him instead as he turns, grabs my hand tightly, and pulls me along with him through this underground world.

Eleven

"WHEN ARE YOU GOING to tell me where we're going?" My voice is raspy with exhaustion. We've been walking for hours. I try to keep my pace equal to Michael's, but I'm struggling.

"You'll see. We're almost there," Michael says calmly, clearly not fazed by the intense exercise.

I always wondered why people enjoyed hiking, but after this jaunt, I totally understand. Even though this pace is unbearable, I do appreciate the landscape and secretly wish we had time to bask in the quiet and enjoy the serenity. I haven't seen any wildlife, which surprises me, but frequently I remind myself that we're still underground. However, there are lovely waterfalls and rivers. The fact that this place is belowground still amazes me. The complexity of the flora is beyond belief. How does the artificial sunlight support all of this? I feel as if I'm experiencing something you would only read about in a science fiction novel.

"Here we are," Michael says with a pleased tone, raising his hands in triumph. "We did good, Alexa. I didn't expect us to cover all that ground in six hours."

I smile, I'm proud of myself, though not completely sure why. "Now what?" A thick green forest surrounds us on all sides. Crisp air cleanses my nose and fills my lungs and I'm briefly transported back to Earth and reminded of my last camping trip a few years ago. Elena and I ventured to Saco River in Maine. We spent a weekend kayaking and camping out. It was an amazing adventure.

"We stay here and get some sleep, then in the morning, we are off."

The silence between us is interrupted by an audible protest from my stomach. Michael's brow furrows in response. "Why didn't you tell me you were hungry?"

"I wasn't until right now."

"I'm going to catch us dinner. You stay here and set up camp." Michael tosses his backpack to me and winks playfully.

"What're you going to catch, exactly? I didn't see anything during our trek." My mouth begins to water thinking about food. I'm starving.

"I'm going down to the river—don't you worry, there are plenty of fish-like animals to eat." He grins. I'm too nervous to ask him to elaborate. Before I can think of a witty comeback, he is gone.

Great, I need to set up camp. I glance to my right and spot a patch of moss, a soft place to camp, I think. I open the backpack to find our sleeping bags from the night before. I try to remember everything Michael had set out. Two bags, a thermos, an additional blanket, beside a campfire. I quickly spread the gear out and make it as inviting as I possibly can. Satisfied, I survey my work. Basically, I've recreated what I remember from yesterday.

I pick up the backpack and make sure I laid out everything that was packed. All of the compartments are empty. I set the bag down at my feet and my eye glimpses a silver zipper on the side. Another compartment. This bag is a camper's dream come true.

I pick the bag up and peer inside the missed compartment. Seeing nothing, I stick my hand inside the cool nylon pouch and pull out a worn photograph. It's a picture of an older man and a little boy. The little boy strongly resembles Michael. Why is this hidden? I'm pretty sure these people in the picture are members of his family. Maybe even his father and brother. I've never met or seen his father on Earth. He also said he was an only child. Who could this be?

Hearing a noise nearby, I jam the photo back into its hidden pocket and zip it shut. Stumbling upon that picture makes me feel like I'm invading Michael's privacy. Obviously, if he wants to share it with me, he will. But why didn't he? He knows all this information about me and it leaves me vulnerable. The least he could do is let me in on something meaningful about him.

"Wow, this place is set up perfectly," Michael comments as he approaches the makeshift camp. I push the unresolved thoughts from my mind and concentrate on the now. He will share his story when he's ready, I secretly hope.

"So we have a few options for dinner." Smiling proudly, Michael lifts a nylon rope with dinner attached. Clearly, there are two different types of fish, types I've never seen before.

"What kind of fish is that?" I kneel down to inspect it closer. I can't believe my eyes. Not only does the slimy green creature have fins, it also has legs and arms! I peer into its black-saucer eyes and see the story of the creature's life unfold: images of it swimming, walking through the forest, and interacting with other beings, all play through my mind like a movie. Dazed, I slowly reach out to touch it. The slimy skin is cool and then hot—so hot it burns me.

Michael is screaming something, but I can't hear what. My ears are buzzing. I fall back onto the ground. I know this scenario all too well. I'm passing out. Again.

"Alexa, what's happening? Where are you?"

The voice rings loud in my head. I can only see darkness, but I know that voice.

"Alexa, you're in danger. Tell me where you're. I'll come to you." Jax's voice is strained and riddled with fear.

"Jax?" I whisper.

"Alexa, are you okay? I had a bad feeling that something happened to you." I can tell Jax is sincerely worried.

"I'm not sure what happened. I...I think I passed out. But I'm okay."

"Where are you? Who are you with?"

"I'm with Michael, a friend. He's protecting me."

"No, Alexa, he's not who you think he is!" Jax's anger and concern are palpable, even in my dreamlike state.

"What do you mean?" I quickly retort.

"He's working for..." Jax's voice fades and I know this means that I'm waking.

"Jax, I can't hear you. Michael is working for who?" I try to listen for a reply, but all that follows is dead silence and complete darkness.

"Alexa, wake up!" Michael's voice is rattling in my head, but I can't move. "Alexa!"

I try to blink in response to his words, but nothing is happening. I'm trapped in my own body. I can hear, think, smell, and sense what's around me, but I can't move. Why is this happening to me?

"Alexa, if you can hear me, relax your body. Take in deep breaths and remain calm." Michael doesn't seem that concerned that I'm in a paralyzed state. Maybe he doesn't know that's what it is, but why else would he be saying this?

I take a few deep breaths and consciously attempt to loosen up. I flutter my eyelashes, and instead of darkness, I see the faint outline of a body, all details in varying shades of gray. I close them again, trying to regroup.

"The sooner you relax, the sooner you'll be able to open your eyes and move." Michael's hand takes mine. His touch helps my body relax.

A few minutes pass. I regain control of my arms and legs. Soon after that, my jaw relaxes enough that I can open and close my mouth. "What happened to me?" I whisper. I keep my eyes closed a few more minutes, almost too embarrassed to open them.

Michael squeezes my hand, I assume in an attempt to make me feel better. "Alexa, I don't know what Kasper has told you, but you're very powerful. If you don't wield the power within you, then the power has the potential to control you."

Tears sting the backs of my eyelids before they stream down my face.

"I know you're afraid," Michael says gently. "This is all so much for you. But I'm here to help you."

His kind words slow the trickle of tears down my face. "Michael, what am I going to do?" I finally open my eyes to see him staring down at me.

"You're not going to do anything. We will get through this. As soon as we leave here, I'm taking you to a very powerful being. She will be able to help guide you. You may actually be from the same bloodline, so she'll be able to tell you more than I can." Michael's smile is reassuring. "We will find the answers."

I sit up, still dizzy, but better than before. "Okay, so what do we do now?"

"We eat! While you were napping, I prepared dinner."

I look behind Michael to see a smoking hole in the ground with our dinner on a rock next to it. "Ha-ha," I drawl. "I wasn't napping." I refocus on the object on the rock. "There's no way I can eat that. What is that thing? It tried to kill me! It used my magic against me."

Michael is laughing so hard, his whole body is shaking. His laugh is contagious. I start to giggle, too.

"Hmm," he muses, frowning in mock concern. "It tastes just like chicken. But I guess I'll have to eat it all myself." He nods toward the fish. "Although if you don't eat, you'll become more susceptible to passing out. It's important to remain well rested and nourished."

"Fine," I concede. "Will it burn me again?" I ask as I move closer.

"No. I tried to warn you, but you were almost in a trance, so you didn't hear me until it was too late." Michael replies. "It burned you because that's how they protect themselves from predators. Green handfish are not only smart, but tasty, too. The trance was your magic's doing."

"Handfish? I've never heard of handfish before—a fish that has not only fins, but arms and legs. Is it native to Pumalia?" My stomach growls as I study our dinner.

"No, it actually once inhabited Mapu, as well, but like many other species, it has become nearly extinct." Michael hands me a piece of the strange meat. I close my eyes and take a bite. "What do you think, do you like it?"

"It's actually not bad. It reminds me of haddock from home." I take another bite and realize just how hungry I am.

After we eat, we both lie on our sleeping bags, enjoying our full bellies and the downtime. Michael's voice breaks the silence. "We should sleep a few hours, and then we'll be off." He shifts his sleeping bag directly next to me.

I crawl into mine, laziness takes over my body. A blanket of fatigue weighs me down. Michael curls up behind me and rests his arm around my waist.

"Goodnight, Alexa," he whispers in my ear, and kisses the top of my head.

"Goodnight, Michael." I quickly fall into a deep, restless sleep. My dream replays Jax's warning about Michael. I find myself confused even in my dream state.

Waking up before Michael does seems odd, but it's also great. Now I can freshen up in the stream before we leave. I get out of my sleeping bag as quietly as possible and take a few steps into the woods toward the last river I remember seeing on our journey here. I turn around to make sure Michael is still asleep. He appears to be. He looks so peaceful. I hold onto that image as I walk through the woods. This underground world is so peacefully quiet, it's almost eerie.

Just as I see the river ahead, I hear something behind me. I smile wide and turn around to yell at Michael for sneaking up on me. No one is there.

I continue a few more steps and enter a clearing, its rocky surface confirming that I'm almost at the river. Rustling in the bushes startles me. I freeze. Something, or someone, is nearby.

More rustling sounds from behind me.

Great, I think, *I'm surrounded.*

My lungs fill with air and I slowly release it telling myself not to panic. If I do, I'll probably pass out.

Maybe if I turn around, I can make it back to Michael before I'm attacked. I halt my strides. Fear paralyzes me. "You're very powerful. Don't be afraid," I whisper to myself.

"You shouldn't be wandering around all by yourself."

The voice immobilizes me. I turn my head slowly to the right, then the left. I see no one.

"For someone with so much power, you're weak."

I close my eyes and try to diffuse my anger by imagining Elena. I refuse to pass out again.

I slowly open my eyes to see a man standing only a foot away from me. He regards me with beady, black eyes that radiate wickedness. The hair on the back of my neck stands taut.

I have nowhere to run.

I gather my courage and study the man. His stature, his eyes, his gray-speckled, black hair remind me of someone.

"Nothing to say, Alexa?" An evil smile splits his pale face.

"What do you want with me?" Hearing my unwavering voice gives me a further sense of strength. I'm not going down without a fight.

"Heh-heh." His chuckle rolls out of his mouth as a low growl. "You clearly have no idea just how important your powers are. There's no one in this galaxy that wouldn't want you, whether to use you for their own gain, or as a bargaining chip. However, my reasons are far less self-centered. I'm here for your mother." The malice drips off his last word.

Why does she want me so badly? "She sent you to get me?"

"No, she sent *me*," a familiar voice says from behind me.

I whip my head around to find Michael standing there. "Makin, why have you come here? I was bringing her to the palace today."

My knees wobble, and what strength I thought I might bring to bear against this man is sucked out of me. Michael's face is uncharacteristically sinister. How can this be the same person that's been taking care of me, kissing me, and holding me? Those thoughts now turn my stomach. I fall to my knees. I have no one to trust; everyone in my life lies and uses me. I don't know who to believe or who I should suspect as a true enemy. I don't want to show him emotion, but the reality of the situation nearly crushes me.

"Well, you were taking your sweet time retrieving her," Makin says. "It was decided that I join you for the journey back."

Michael tugs at my arm to get me up.

"Leave me alone!" I yell.

His once welcoming eyes are now dark and distant. The Michael I knew is gone. "Fine, do it yourself. Get up. We're leaving."

His frosty reply only digs the knife deeper into my gut. How could I believe he was here for me? How stupid can I be? First Jax, and now Michael. I feel my heart crumbling inside me as I push myself to my feet.

"Where's the craft?" Michael asks Makin.

Makin waves his hand upward. "It's hidden above ground. No one will see it."

"Good. This doesn't change the deal we've made, Makin. I've done everything you've asked. I was bringing her to you today." Michael's voice is stern, but there's an edge of desperation in it.

"Of course not, Michael. The queen will release them upon our arrival." Makin sends me a diabolical glare. "She'll be very pleased to see that you found her." He tips his head back and lets out a menacing laugh.

Michael grabs his bag and herds me toward the dark man. "Lead the way, Makin," he commands.

"It's just this way." Makin takes the lead, which leaves me in the middle.

Twelve

THE ARTIFICIAL LIGHT IS fading, and with each passing minute, the shadows grow larger. I know it's close to the simulated nighttime when our true forms are revealed. Anxiety builds within me, boiling to the surface. What will this dark man look like in his true form?

The nervous energy swirls around inside me, searching for a way out. My hands start to tingle, warning me that it's only a matter of time before they do something I cannot control.

The plant life suddenly comes alive and shifts, first moving in place, then coming toward us. As the mass gets closer, I realize it isn't the plants that are moving. There are little green-winged men flying in our direction. The buzzing from their flapping wings is nearly deafening. The wind from their passage whips across my face, making it hard for me to keep my eyes open.

"They know we're here; we must move quickly," Makin shouts over the buzzing.

Michael grabs my arm and starts to run, towing me behind him like a rag doll. I know I don't want to go with them, but a glance behind me confirms that there's no way I want to stay and chat with these little green men.

"Michael, I can't keep up with you," I cry, barely hearing my own voice over the humming in my ears.

He glances over his shoulder and, for a moment, his eyes meet mine. I can't hear him, but I can read his lips. "I'm sorry." Then he turns his face away and pulls me harder as he picks up his pace.

My head starts to throb. What does he mean, he's sorry? He tricks me and is handing me over to the woman whom I've been protected from all these years, the woman he was just bashing for ruining the galaxy, and he's sorry?

Makin interrupts my train of thought when he shrieks, "We're almost there! This way, hurry!"

We come to a huge mountain of rock. It's far too high to climb, and it has to be a dead end. But then Makin turns sideways and shimmies through an opening, disappearing into the crevasse in the rock.

Michael gently pushes me in front of him and urges me to move quickly through the cleft. I close my eyes and slide through. I open my eyes only to see darkness, but I just keep moving toward a pinhole of light I finally see in front of me. The sharp rock walls nip at my back as I sidle along, but I stay focused.

I sidestep through the crack for what seems forever. I can tell we've gone uphill a bit, but that's all I know for sure.

Taking the last few steps through the passage toward the light is a relief. We emerge into a giant clearing with a huge, round, metal object in its center.

As we approach the object, a door opens and stairs extend down to the ground. Makin stops and ushers Michael and I up, then quickly follows us. The steps fold up and the metal door slams shut behind us. I immediately know that this is a flying saucer. I've heard of people claiming to have seen these back home, but I never believed they were real—until now.

The inside is a light, shiny silver that's almost blinding, but my eyes adjust quickly—too quickly. I assume this is a special alien power within me; if I were a human, this would probably blind me.

I examine the interior, but there isn't much to see. The smooth, seamless walls contain panels with switches, levers, and buttons of all shapes, sizes, and colors. The middle of the saucer has three rows of white bucket seats.

"Sit, Alexa!" Makin shouts and disappears toward the front, where there's a huge tinted window and a large chair.

I sit in a bucket seat and harness myself in. I think back to the tiny, car-like spacecraft Jax brought me here in. It's almost comical compared to this monstrosity.

Michael appears next to me. He doesn't say a word. He won't even meet my gaze. He checks my safety harness and sits down next to me. I stare straight ahead, not wanting to see his face. But I can't help the tears building up in my eyes; it's only a matter of time before they spill out. I sense his gaze on me, but I stubbornly keep my focus on a spot ahead of me, unseeing, uncaring. Pissed.

"Michael, come help me," Makin calls from the pilot's chair.

Michael rises and goes forward. I can hear Makin barking orders at him, but I can't make out exactly what he's saying.

Why would Michael do this to me? Why would he pretend to like me if he was just going to betray me? Too exhausted to cry, I close my eyes and slump against the back of the seat. I try to imagine why Michael would do this, but nothing comes to mind. I truly believed he liked me. How stupid can I be?

Somewhere between thinking about Michael and feeling the spacecraft lift off, my eyelids become very heavy.

The journey through the woods and Michael's deceit have taken their toll, and I can't fight the drug-induced slumber that my body craves.

When I come to, I can tell that the silver saucer is still in the air. I look around, but I can't see Michael or the evil puppetmaster, Makin. I undo my harness and slowly stand. The floor moves beneath me as if I'm in an elevator. I quickly get used to the sensation and start to move about, wanting to see exactly what I'm facing.

It's eerily quiet and calm. I take careful shuffling steps toward the front where I saw them both right before takeoff, but no one is there. However, I'm mesmerized by the view through the giant window in front of me.

It's just like the movies, but better. The blackness of space is illuminated by sparkling diamonds—stars. I assume they're stars, but I've never seen one up close like this. The spacecraft moves at a steady pace. I watch objects outside the window disappear as quickly as they appear.

The only giant object that remains in the window is a large mass—a planet, I assume—right in front of me. The saucer is headed straight for it. Its grand size intimidates me. Brilliant-orange, planetary rings similar to those circling Saturn encompass the purple-hued planet. To the right of the planet there are three orange-red objects lined up in a row. At this distance, they look similar to Earth's moon. That image is shockingly familiar to me. My mind starts to spin and I feel nauseous. I close my eyes and rest my head in my hands. These are the same moons I've been seeing in my dreams. The same ones I saw on Pumalia, as well.

Even though my eyes are closed, I can sense Michael coming toward me. I jump a bit when I open my eyes and see him staring at me. He isn't cold and expressionless like he was before. The way he leans in against the chair, I can tell he's more relaxed.

"Go back to your chair before he sees you," he whispers sternly. I guess I was wrong; his voice *is* emotionless. The Michael I knew is really gone.

"What do you care? You turned me over to him." I try to make my voice equally cold.

Michael shakes his head as if my words have slapped him across the face. I think I accomplished my goal.

Trying not to show my confusion and despair, I slowly walk back to my chair. It seems his gaze burns a hole through my back.

"What's she doing up?" Makin asks Michael as he enters.

"She was just stretching her legs," Michael answers coolly.

I want to speak up and tell him that he's going to pay. I want to scare him in a way that will let him know that he made a big mistake. But all I can do is build on the anger growing inside me. No longer am I scared, sad, or hurt. Instead, I'm becoming enraged.

Tingling starts at my fingertips and moves quickly up my arms. I know this feeling is a warning I typically get before flames emerge from my nails. I try to calm myself by counting to ten, accompanied by deep breathing.

Makin notices I'm acting weird because I can hear him move closer. "What's she doing? I thought you said she didn't have any abilities yet." His voice is tight with anxiety.

I can hear Michael's breathing quicken. "I said it's too early to tell. She hasn't shown any signs of them yet." Michael is lying—he knows damn well about my abilities. Why would he lie?

The tension in the air quadruples while I'm in my counting trance. When I blink my eyes open, I see both of them standing before me with their mouths open, gawking at me. I know without even confirming my suspicion that my fingers are lit up like Christmas trees.

"She needs to be restrained." Makin's voice trembles. He reaches into his oversized, brown robe and pulls out a needle. I know there's nothing I can do to avoid being stuck. He has me cornered against my seat. And where am I going to run in this tin can, anyway?

Michael tries to comfort me—I think. "This won't hurt, Alexa. It will make you sleepy and more comfortable until we reach our destination."

I want to believe him, but it was only yesterday that he was holding me while I slept, and today he's aiding in my capture for the queen.

I clench my teeth and take the shot like a woman. My body instantly surrenders to the drug and there's nothing I can do but slouch to the deck. Having totally lost all control, I have no way to stop my head from colliding with the shiny white surface. The last thing I remember is a loud bang and pain as my head bounces off the floor.

"Jax! Help me! They have taken me," I scream as loud as I can in my drug-induced coma. My mind is slowly darkening and I know the mental connection will soon be severed, but I wait to hear something, anything.

No response. There's nothing I can do except succumb. For now I'll try and rest.

Rest doesn't find me. Instead, the sounds of my own screams violently jar me from my brief state of unconsciousness. Chills flow down my spine, shaking my body. My eyes throb behind my closed lids, and the thought of opening them is draining. I don't move or make another sound, but I can still hear the echo of my screams reverberating throughout the room.

My legs ache, my stomach hurts, and my arms feel crushed. The side of my body that meets the cool floor beneath me is slick with sweat. My hands are tightly fastened behind my back. How can this be happening to me again? I thought Michael was my friend—even more than a friend.

His face is the last image I see before the drugs take me back on a dark journey into my unconscious.

Moments later I wake again. Slowly, I open my eyes. The air burns them as I try to focus on my surroundings. Struggling to sit upright, I notice I'm alone. I madly scan the tiny room that holds me captive, looking for a possible escape route. But there's nothing, not even a door or window. I feel panic rising. Will I have enough air to live? Does anyone know I'm here? My heart sinks to the pit of my empty stomach. How can he betray me like this? Michael is supposed to be my kind hero, coming to save me.

He was my first kiss.

I close my eyes and find a safe place within, "One, two, three, four..." The deep inhalations soothe the parts of me that want to break down.

One thought has me curious: if I'm so badass and everyone wants me, then I must be able to get out of here, or at the very least, tell Jax where I am so he can come and help me.

Calmness takes over and the rigidness in my body dissolves. I reach into my subconscious and look for a way to make contact with Jax. The only thing I can find fresh in my mind is the memories of the dreams I've had with him. I try to relive my time in the field of purple-stemmed flowers, but no luck. I even picture Jax in my living room, then in his small car-like spacecraft, but all of the memories are, in fact, only memories. Nothing is giving me that tingling that I get when I make contact with him.

I continue to focus on him, to hone in in on his features. The mental picture comforts me. I feel like I've known Jax for a long time. Most nights I dreamed of him, and most days I daydreamed about him.

Relentlessly, I call his name mentally, over and over again, but there's no response. I'm not sure how long I sit there trying to connect with him, because eventually, I fall asleep out of pure exhaustion.

"Alexa, Alexa, where are you?" Jax's voice sounds strained and surreal.

But I'm so happy to hear him, either way. "Jax?" I draw in a lungful of air and hold it, waiting to hear his response. I look around, but all I see is darkness. No dream. I squint my eyes, hoping to catch a glimpse of him.

"Listen, Alexa, I'm coming for you. Please, don't do anything stupid. These beings want to keep you and your powers. They are very dangerous." I can hear the intensity in his voice. His blue eyes flash in my mind; I wish I could see all of him.

"Jax, I'm sorry I left without telling you. I just thought that was the only way." Even though my eyes are shut, tears dampen my face. Guilt consumes me. He's still looking for me, even though I ran away from him.

"Alexa, don't worry about that now. I'm coming, and I'm very close." His voice is fading quickly into the dark abyss.

"Jax! Jax, are you there?"

Only silence follows my pleas.

I allow myself to continue to weep for my poor judgment, my mistakes, for Elena, for Jax, and for the person I thought Michael was.

Thirteen

"GET AWAY FROM ME, Michael!" I stare at the floor, not wanting to give him the satisfaction of looking at him. I don't want him to see how deeply he has wounded me. Michael's hot breath tickles my ear. I can feel him loosen the restraints behind my back and gently brush the hair out of my face.

Michael sits back and draws in a breath. "Alexa, you don't understand, and I can't tell you, but you have to believe me when I say I care about you."

I can't help the laughter that rolls out of my mouth. "Care about me? You kidnapped me and turned me over to the queen's guard to take me to her. You think that's something you do when you care about someone?" The laughing continues, and I'm afraid of what will follow it. "Not to mention drugging me and tying me up. Yeah, I can tell you truly care about me." The sarcasm drips from my words and I know he understands just how much he has hurt me.

"I don't expect you to understand. But I need you to know I had no choice." He shifts his gaze away from me and stares at the wall.

I can see the pain clouding his big, brown eyes, but I don't want to see it. He did this to me—I *have* to remember that.

With an exaggerated sigh, he meets my eyes. "And back home, those feelings were real—I mean they *are* real. But I have to suppress them or they'll keep me away from you. I'm working on a plan for all of us. I need to save them, too."

"Save who?" I reply, bewildered by this cryptic revelation. Who would he have to save besides me?

Before he can respond, the door opens. "Oh, I'm glad to see the princess is awake." Makin grins. "It's time to make yourself pretty so you can visit with the queen." The smug expression on his face makes my stomach turn.

"Makin, she still seems groggy to me. I think we should let her sleep off the drugs so we can ensure a proper meeting between the two." Michael's eyes darken and go cold, heartless. The light I saw moments before Makin's arrival is now extinguished.

"Oh, Michael, she'll have plenty of time to rest once she meets the queen and her abilities are formally bound. These makeshift, enchanted bonds won't last forever." Makin chuckles and exits the room.

"I'm sorry," Michael whispers right before two armed guards come in.

The tallest of the two men stare me squarely in the eyes and says, "Princess, you can walk or we can carry you—which is it going to be?" His bald head is shiny, and the glare from the reflected light makes me squint.

"I'll walk, but I need someone to untie me so I can get up." I must appear strong and fearless. The last thing I want is for Michael to see me fall apart. I need him to know that I can do this without his help.

"We will not untie you, but we will certainly help you up," the shorter man with wild, curly, red hair says, reaching down and grabbing my arm to pull me to my feet. I turn to glare at him and shoot him a scathing thank-you, but his hard eyes silence me.

Another man enters the room and quietly speaks to Michael. All I can make out is something about the queen, and wanting to see Michael. The color drains from his face and his body stiffens before he shoots me an odd expression and nods. "Princess," he says by way of farewell, then he's gone.

The tall guard motions toward the door. "Princess, this way, please." I hold my head high and walk out of the room.

I expect a dark, gloomy setting, but when I emerge from the room, I'm taken aback by my new surroundings. Floor-to-ceiling windows, all open, line both sides of the broad corridor. For a moment, the rolling green hills and rich scenery seem like paradise.

"Where are we?" I ask, my voice barely audible even to myself. But I can't hide my awe. On my right, the green flora meets a sandy beach that, in turn, meets sea-green waves, their caps frothed white. I feel as if I've been whisked away to a Caribbean island, not transported flying-saucer-style to a foreign planet.

The intoxicating, warm breeze tickles my face and fills my nose with salty, sweet scents. I'm reluctant to leave the picturesque surroundings behind, but I'm forced to when we enter a large, white room with high ceilings and small, circular windows. Exotic artwork adorns the walls, creating a contemporary vibe that I, for sure, was not expecting.

"Princess, please wait here. Her Highness will be with you shortly." Before I can answer or plead for him to take me with him, the guard and his bald cohort are gone.

I drop down on one knee, trying to calm my nerves by filling my lungs and holding the air in, but the image of Elena keeps flashing through my head. *She* is my mom, not some queen that's ruining the galaxy and wreaking havoc.

Part of me worries that this encounter will reveal a truth that I've always sensed. Maybe that constant, nagging of not belonging, and waiting for something big to happen, is finally happening. Deep down, I've sensed that I've been living a lie, and today might be the day the truth is revealed.

Before I can give it another thought, the door flies open. The two guards who escorted me here enter first, with Makin following. They form an awkward line and kneel down on one knee. My heart starts to pound in my chest, its thudding echoing faintly in my ears. I know this is a precursor to passing out, but I fight the urge to give in like a helpless child. This is a time when I need to show my strength, not pass out like some swooning twit.

"Princess, bow your head to the queen," Makin growls, scowling at me.

I long to reply with a snide remark, but instead, I bow my head. As soon as I do, the air in the room goes still.

"Please, rise. There is no need for formalities in front of my daughter, though she's a princess." Her voice isn't what I'd imagined it would be. She sounds soft-spoken and calm.

"Daughter, finally we meet. I've been searching for you for seventeen years." She draws in a long breath and exhales. "Please, look at me, Alexa."

Slowly, I raise my head to meet her gaze. The first thing I notice is her large, piercing, purple eyes. She has wavy blonde hair that falls to just below her shoulders, reminding me of my own hair color on Earth.

"Alexa, are you well? Have they hurt or mistreated you?"

Is she actually worried about me? "I-I'm okay. Just very confused." It comes out in a whisper.

"I'm sure you are. Let's get you washed up and in some new clothes. I'll explain everything. Gabe, Gavin, show her to her room. Get her a snack and prepare Aria." Even though she speaks softly, you can tell that the people in the room are wary—attentive and hanging on her every movement.

"Yes, Your Majesty," the bald guard replies. The three of them kneel once more, and as quickly as she came, she's gone. I'm left there completely bewildered.

The bald guard comes toward me. "This way, Princess." He motions in the direction of the door and I oblige. I need to figure out where I am—and who I am.

I spin and ask the guard, "So, are you Gabe, or Gavin?"

"I'm Gavin." His face remains expressionless.

Gabe almost knocks me over when he darts past me to the door. He opens it and waves me through with a gentlemanly sweep of his hand. As I walk across the threshold, Gabe bows his head. These are the same guards who found me in that room, and probably the ones who put me there. Could all this be true? Am I truly a princess? Because they sure have changed their tune in the short time the queen has addressed me.

"This way, Princess," Gavin says proudly.

I was beginning to think we were aimlessly wandering around, until I hear his voice. I felt as if we were traveling in circles, but when I questioned Gavin, he confirmed that the castle is, indeed, a maze-like fortress with a lot of rooms.

The guards halt at a tall, blue, glass door. "This is it, Princess. This is your chamber." Gavin gestures toward the portal.

I gently lean against it and turn the sparkling crystal knob, pushing it open on "my chamber." My breath catches in my throat. The tall, A-frame ceiling is adorned with at least twenty oval windows. The walls are a pale, sea-green with more windows—*giant* ones—overlooking a pink-sand beach.

In the center of the room is a huge bed. It appears even larger than Sheri's parents' bed. They have a king-size bed, and I always wondered what it would be like to spread out on a bed that big after being so used to a twin bed. The blankets are a crisp white, and they appear to be soft, even fluffy. That is the moment I realize just how tired I am.

"Gavin, this room is for me?" My voice sounds small and insecure, but the grandeur of this "chamber" makes me feel out of place.

"Yes, Princess. When the queen found out that you were, in fact, alive, she had this wing of the castle designed for you." Gavin goes to the windows and presses a button. Blinds whir down from inside the ceiling, immediately darkening the room. "Why don't you take a bath and rest for a while? Gabe will be outside your door if you need anything. I'll come for you in a few hours, right before dinner."

"Um, okay." Before I can ask any questions, they quickly exit the room.

Walking around the room, I find a double door with large, silver handles. I pull one handle toward me, opening a closet full of silk gowns in every color. The door next to it opens into a shoe closet. There are shelves of high heels, slippers, and sandals, closed-toe and open-toe shoes in every color imaginable. I pick up a pair of glittery, silver slippers and try one on. A perfect fit. How could all of these shoes be in my size?

I step back and look around. What does this mean? Why do I have a room and closets full of clothes and shoes in my size? Why is the vicious queen being so nice? Can she really be my mother? These thoughts tangle in my head until it feels as though I'm trying to think through a foggy haze. I stumble to the bed, sit down, and rest my head in my hands.

Elena, Michael, Jax, Makin, the queen—their faces swim behind my eyelids. How can this be happening to me? This is all too crazy to actually be true. I try to focus and replay the events of the past few days in my head, but I'm missing something. How did so many people fool me? My mind goes around in circles. People's faces, brief memories, but the question still lingers...who's for real and who's lying?

Fourteen

I FIND MYSELF LYING in the field of purple-stemmed flowers. The sky above me is a faint pink, scattered with twinkling stars. They appear so close. I bring my hand up to touch them even though they're a great distance away. The three looming moons are now blood red, which sends a shiver down my spine. Usually in my dreams, the moons are brilliant yellow, not dark and dreadful.

"Alexa!" His voice sings in my ear. I knew he'd be searching for me.

"Jax, where are you? Where am I? What's happening?" I sit up and explore my surroundings, but there's no sign of him.

"I'm close by. Are you in the field?" His voice is tense and throaty, as if he's been running.

"I am." My body starts to tingle in anticipation at seeing Jax again. I'm both happy to see him and angry with him for bringing me to Pumalia and endangering Elena.

Jax emerges from the tree line. His tall, muscular figure is unmistakable. As he approaches, I notice he isn't wearing his uniform, but instead a tight, white shirt and gray sweatpants. His piercing-blue eyes radiate concern and worry.

"Are you okay? What have they done to you?" He kneels down beside me and gently takes my hand in his. I quickly pull back, not knowing how I feel about him, about what he has done to me. However, the sparks are undeniable; they travel up my arm from the spot where he touched my hand. "Alexa, I'm so sorry. I never imagined any of this would happen. You have to believe that."

"Jax, I don't know what I believe. You took me from my home and delivered me to a prison. Elena could be hurt—or even worse—for helping me escape." I didn't mean to talk so loudly, but I can't hide the hurt and I need to blame someone.

He turns away and studies his hands. "I know. I would have a hard time believing me, too. But Elena is okay. Maddox imprisoned her, but I helped her escape; she's safe now."

"All those dreams of mine that you've been in, and you never warned me. Why didn't you tell me about all of this? Why didn't you warn me?" Tears prick the back of my eyes, but I fight them off. I don't need to appear even more vulnerable than I already feel.

"It's not that easy, Alexa. There has always been a way to do things, and I was following protocol. I had no reason—until the end—to question Maddox." The sincerity in his voice speaks volumes, and at that moment, I know he's being honest. "I wasn't aware who your parents were, but I never know those details. I just help acquire half-breeds and bring them to Pumalia. That's always been part of my job."

We both sit there in silence. "I did know something was different with you," he says quietly. "I've never communicated so much with someone in a dream state. Typically, I meet the being a day or two before their birthday and ease them into the transition, a transition that they're well aware of. But you never knew what was happening—and you were always there. Just like now. How do you come here? I fall asleep and I hear you calling me, and before I know it, I'm here in the field or forest. It's like we have a connection. I've never experienced this before." His expression mirrors my confusion.

"How do I do it? I don't do anything!" Anger spikes in my blood, but I don't want to explode in front of Jax.

He stares up at the sky, appearing mesmerized by the moons. "I'm sorry if you thought I was accusing you of knowing what's going on. I just thought maybe you somehow knew how to get here. Every time I've visited with you in your dream, we seem to meet here. I've never been here before. Usually with other integrations, we meet in their Earth home, or on Pumalia at the compound."

A flicker of jealousy creeps through my body. "You've done this a lot, with others like me?"

His stoic face cracks a grin while he's contemplating my question. "I would never say that the other half-breeds are anything like you."

"So, how am I different—besides the different dreamland meeting place?" I want him to say that I'm not that different, that I'm not a freak in my Earth life or here in this galaxy.

"Well, first of all, I'm usually able to tell you everything about you when I first meet you in the dream world. But I was given little information on you, and when I queried, Maddox told me you were a risk. I wasn't supposed to tell you anything. As I got to know you, I couldn't figure out why he would say those things. Now it all makes sense—he was afraid of you and didn't want me to endanger him."

"So he's afraid of me because of who my parents are? Or what powers I might have?" I snort out loud. My powers don't seem to be doing me any good right now.

"Well, yes—both. He's afraid that your father will come out of hiding and hunt him down. He's afraid of your mother because of the war she's waging against the galaxy." Jax shifts his gaze back to his fidgeting hands, hiding his beautiful blue eyes.

"I don't think he has to worry about my father—I don't think he'll be coming for me. If he could leave me with Elena for the first fourteen years of my life, then I doubt he'll be searching for me now." The idea that my father has been alive my whole life isn't only disturbing, but sad. When Elena told me that my father was gone and "watching us from above," then I at least knew he didn't leave me by choice. But now that's changed.

I go from having one parent to no parent, to having both birth parents alive and dysfunctional. I thought life was tough before when I was the odd girl out, but now I yearn for that simple life.

"Alexa, are you okay?" His voice pulls me from my thoughts. I'm thankful.

"Sure, I'm great!" I say with a little too much irony and excitement.

Jax gifts me with a teasing, sidelong glance and a charming smile. "It seems you are."

"Well, before I disappear and wake up, what should I do about the queen? She honestly doesn't seem so terrible." My face heats because I remember hearing the awful acts she's allegedly committed. Part of me wants to anger Jax; I'm not sure why, though.

"She's not bad. Aside from killing innocent beings, or locking away beings' loved ones for no reason other than to satisfy her hunger for terrorizing the innocent, not to mention trying to kill your father in an ambush that she orchestrated, she's a great queen." The sarcasm and disgust drip from his words, and my heart sinks.

"I'm sorry, I didn't mean it to sound—"

Before I can properly take back what I said, the landscape starts to fade. The tingling in my limbs signifies I'm being yanked back into my unnatural reality. "Jax, please come for me."

He leans in and kisses my forehead. His lips leave a burning sensation that warms my whole body. "I'm going to find you, Alexa, I promise."

His exquisite eyes find mine and I let myself vanish without a fight.

"Let her be. She's had a long journey and she needs to rest."

I know that voice all too well. It's Michael's. I hear the door open and close with a *whoosh-click*. Why would he care if I'm rested or not? He all but captured me and brought me to this place.

Voices murmur in the background as I emerge from my dream reunion with Jax. "Oh good, she's finally waking up now," a girl whispers close by.

My eyelids flutter, finally opening. A young girl is hovering above me, staring. Long, brown hair frames her pale, oval face. Her large, almond-shaped, lilac eyes blink as the corners of her mouth move into an excited smile. "Finally, you're awake! I've been waiting days to meet you."

"Um, how long have I been sleeping?" I start to sit up and whip the warm blankets off of me, but I stop when I realize I have no pants on. How did I even get under the blankets or into these clothes?

Confusion must be written all over my face. She kneels on the bed in front of me, trying not to laugh. "You have been sleeping for two days. I actually came to visit you the first night you were here, but you fell asleep on the bed. So I got you into your pajamas and covered you up. I didn't think you would mind, since we're sisters and all."

"I'm sorry, it sounded like you said...wait a minute. Did you say you—you're my...my *sister*? How can that be? Is this some sort of joke?"

"You surely ask a lot of questions." She giggles, reminding me of a young, carefree girl. I can't help but smile a little myself. "Yes, you have a younger half sister— well not that young. I'm twelve years old. But I don't think of you as a half. You're my sister, and I've been waiting a few days to meet you. I have always wanted a sister!"

Her excitement is contagious; I smile in return.

She jumps off the bed and traipses to the closet. She's a little shorter than me and her hair is a beautiful light-brown shade. She opens the closet doors and takes out a robe. "Here you go, Alexa. This will keep you warm. Let's go eat some breakfast! By the way, my name is Miri."

"I still have so many questions." The weight of what has transpired makes me tremble. "I need answers—I need to know why I'm here, and where here is."

She hands me the fluffy, pink robe and I quickly wrap my shivering body in it. The trembling ceases before I tie the robe closed. It's the softest, warmest robe I have ever felt.

Miri quickly walks to the door. "Hurry up, Alexa, before the cooks start making lunch. I'll answer as many questions as I can after breakfast." She holds the door open and I promptly follow her.

I didn't realize how hungry I am. My grumbling stomach makes Miri giggle uncontrollably all the way to the kitchen. I can't help but giggle myself; her happiness is contagious.

The kitchen is unbelievably huge. An army of cooks is prepping food, wielding an equally huge array of kitchen appliances and gadgets. Miri weaves around the cooks to a bank of cupboards, then refrigerators, then tables covered in trays of food. She comes back to where I'm waiting at a table tucked away in a nook. She's bearing two plates loaded with pancakes, fresh fruit, and yogurt with granola. I feel like we're on Earth, enjoying breakfast out at a diner.

We immediately dig in to our plates. "Mmmm, this is delicious. Thank you for bringing me down here for breakfast." My stomach fills up fast because I haven't eaten in some time. The meal makes me think of my Earth life and what Elena probably had in store for me for my birthday breakfast.

"No problem. I figured you'd want to avoid as many beings as possible, considering what has happened and who you are." Miri is finally slowing down, and instead of shoveling forkful after forkful of food into her mouth, she uses her fork to roll around the few grapes and cherries left on her plate.

"So, now that we're done with breakfast, are you going to answer my questions?" I don't mean to be rude, but I need to know what's happening—and now.

She smiles and whispers, "Of course, but not here—there are too many people lurking around."

"Okay, where shall we go?" I realize we won't be going anywhere but back to my room when I remember what I'm wearing. "Never mind, clearly I can't go anywhere in this thing."

"Oh, that?" She waves a dismissive hand. "That's an easy fix." Miri peeks over her shoulder, presumably to see if anyone is watching us. She whispers a few indiscernible words, and just like that, my robe is gone and I'm in black pants, a purple tunic, and sneakers.

"Wow. That's amazing! How did you do that?" I exclaim, peering at myself in disbelief.

"Oh, that's nothing. You should see what *you're* capable of. You would put that little chant to shame." She shoots up from her seat and takes our plates to the dishwasher. "Follow me, sister—I mean Princess," she says when she returns.

I trail her down a set of stairs to a door that leads outside. I can hear a few giggles escape her even though she's walking in front of me. Miri gently places her hand on the door and it sails open.

"How did you do that?" I blurt, but the wind whipping around outside carries my voice away.

"You mean this?" She holds up her hands and the wind grows stronger. She closes her eyes and spins around wildly in the breeze. I watch in awe as her long hair clings to her face. The wind comes to an immediate standstill when she stops spinning. I stand there with my mouth hanging open.

"You can do this, too." She chuckles and walks toward the water.

I run after her. "Wait, I can do this? I've the same powers as you?" I know I have some sort of something going on, but I never imagined I could do something so controlled as I just witnessed Miri do.

"I told you, we're half sisters. Of course you can do that—our father's parents were very powerful." She looks hopeful and sad all at the same time.

"Wait, the queen isn't your mother?" My own voice echoes in my head. *Why is she here?*

"No, silly, she's the queen and you're the princess. I'm here for you. Well, and the queen made me come here when she found out who I was. But it hasn't been terrible. She's taken care of me since I was three years old. She even lets my mom visit on special occasions, like my birthday."

I can see the sadness in her eyes, and now I realize why. She misses her mom. "Can you leave?"

"No. If I do, they'll hurt my mother. I stay here and do as I'm told. It really isn't that bad." Quickly, she turns and looks at something in the distance. "This is my favorite part of the island," she says, changing the subject.

"We're on an island?" I try to process this new information as I continue to speak. "The rolling green hills, sandy dunes, the serene water—it's all beautiful. I see why you like it out here. I never expected to see this anywhere but at home—I mean Earth." The thought of Earth makes me long for the normalcy I once dreaded.

"Yes, we're on an island. The most beautiful island around." Miri stares off, clearly somewhere else in her mind.

"Miri, can you explain this place to me? I'm still perplexed as to where I actually am." I hear the confusion and desperation in my voice. Not knowing where I am makes me feel powerless—plus, if I know, I can tell Jax the next time I see him in my dreams.

Miri's eyes light up at my request and a smile spreads across her face. She's always smiling. I wonder how she became such a positive young girl. Obviously, her circumstances are less than favorable. It's like she knows something I don't. "Well, what do you want to know, exactly?" Her happy voice squeaks.

"How far are we from Earth? How can I breathe here? Is this planet like Earth? Why haven't scientists on Earth talked about Pumalia or Mapu?" My face starts to heat when I realize Miri is sitting in front of me, trying not to conceal her laughter. "I'm sorry, I'm just really confused."

"Don't be! I don't know what I'd do if I was you. Finding out about this place and then who your parents are, that's crazy."

"Yes, it is," I comment wryly.

"Okay, so now you're in the Magna galaxy. This galaxy is far away from Earth; I think something like fifty-seven billion light years away. That's why scientists on Earth have not identified this galaxy or the planets within it. Also, most of the planets in this galaxy are rocky planets like Earth—life is easily sustainable on these types of planets. You can breathe here because the composition of the air is much like what you're used to on Earth. Plus, you can breathe here without a problem because one of your parents is from here—so you already have the ability to survive here. It's how I can—my mother is from here." Miri lets out a deep sigh and looks up into the sky.

"Our father is from Pumalia, so that's why you had no problem there, either," she adds.

I sense loneliness in her. Usually, Miri is giggly and happy, but at the mention of our father, her whole demeanor changes. "Thanks, Miri. Knowing that much helps me wrap my head around this place."

Before I can say any more, she angles toward me. "What's Earth like?" Her lilac eyes twinkle in the light, and her smile drives the longing from her face.

"Earth isn't much different than what I've experienced here. Except that all the beings are human, and I doubt they have magical powers like us."

She giggles and we continue our walk on the sandy beach. I learn that she's been in an educational program at the castle, which reminds me of homeschooling because she's the only student. However, the material she learns about sounds far more interesting and advanced than what I've been forced to learn.

She tells me about the intergalactic war and the rival families. She speaks of the Council, which the queen now heads, but she doesn't say much more concerning her life, and I'm not going to push the topic.

I also learn that Pumalia and Mapu are embroiled in a separate war that started after the galaxy's war, and that beings from both sister planets have been fleeing to other planets, or they have gone into hiding—like to Aurora, I assume—because they fear the New War and the destruction it will cause. Basically, my mother wants to rule over Pumalia and use its resources for Mapu.

Miri also tells me all about her mother, and how she's a seamstress—I think she would be considered a fashion designer if we were on Earth. The guards deliver letters between her and her mother. I think that's sweet. I can tell from my brief interaction with Gabe and Gavin that the guards aren't all that bad.

"What about Makin? He seems awful." Even though I try, I can't keep the disgust I harbor toward him from my voice.

"Well, I try to stay away from him. He's not nice, and he uses people the same way she does. Please stay away from him, Alexa—he truly is evil." Her posture shrinks and her voice quivers at the very mention of his name.

"Do you know Michael? I think he may work for Makin." An overwhelming sense of sadness runs through me as I picture the brown-haired boy who once wanted to take me to the dance. Or the boy who saved me from Pumalia. Or worse yet, my very first kiss with the boy who betrayed me and handed me over to Makin.

"I know Michael. He's the one who talked the queen into letting my mother visit on my birthday. He's nice, but I know you might not think so because you think he tricked you, right?"

My eyes start to water because I truly don't know who Michael is. "Yes, he did trick me. I thought he liked me, but it was all a ruse to get me here." I bite my bottom lip, creating a painful diversion so I don't cry over him again.

Miri places her hand on mine and smiles. "I'm sorry this has happened to you, Alexa. You must be so confused and sad."

Her small gesture is so very comforting and meaningful at a time like this. Biting my lip isn't working. I can't hold back my inevitable tears. Once they start, I know it will be hard, if not impossible, to stop. However, I don't try—I let myself cry and be comforted by my little sister.

Fifteen

THE WALK BACK TO the castle is peaceful. I enjoy the beautiful scenery and listen to Miri's stories. She has the ability to talk and talk. She tells me all about the guards and how Gavin and Gabe will sometimes sneak chocolate cake to her room when she's having a tough day. The picture she paints of this place doesn't seem as bad as I had imagined.

As we round the corner toward the castle, Michael comes into view. I quickly look out to the ocean, not wanting to make eye contact. But he stops in front of me.

"Alexa, can we speak for a moment?" His voice sounds more authoritative than friendly or familiar.

"Princess, I must go get cleaned up before dinner." Miri curtsies and runs off before I can stop her. I wonder why she's so formal all of the sudden.

"So you not only kidnap people, you scare them off, as well?" The biting words escape my lips before I can stop them.

"Alexa, it's not like that. I had no choice. If it wasn't me, it would have been someone else chosen by Maddox and your mother."

His words rip my attention from the beach and throw me back into my new reality. My mother has kidnapped me from a planet where I had already been taken under false pretenses.

"Well, you didn't have to go so far as to pretend to rescue me and be my Prince Charming. For that matter, why did you pretend to care for me? Why the deceit?" The anger writhes inside me. I hate feeling like a joke.

"They took my family." His eyes bore a hole into me. They're moist with unshed tears.

"Oh." I remember him saying he had to save them—"them" must be his family. I don't have any words for him, or for this unbearable situation.

He reaches into his pocket and hands me the crinkled photo I had found in his backpack while setting up the camp. "This is my father and my little brother, Jonah. They were taken last year when Makin first approached me with this job. I had no choice." He looks down at his hands when he speaks to me.

"I'm sorry this happened to you, but you could have told me. I would have helped you. Instead, you used me. You pretended to like me, and I started to really like you." My bottom lip trembles and I sense the tears will come soon if I don't get away from him.

He sighs and twines his fingers with mine. "Alexa, please believe me when I tell you that I wasn't pretending." Tears fill his big, beautiful eyes just enough so they don't spill over.

Part of me wants to believe him, but a bigger part of me wants to run from him. "Michael, I can't do this right now. I don't know who I can trust—if anybody at all. In the past few days, I've learned I'm not human, I was hidden on Earth by my father—who was thought to be dead, but isn't—my mother is a mad queen, I have a half sister, and I'm once again held captive in a place I don't know." I pull back my hand. "I forgot—I also have magical, coveted powers that for some reason aren't working now." Saying it out loud makes me want to laugh. This just can't be my life.

I take a step back. Giving myself some space away from him allows me to clear my mind and breathe. "Was your family released after you brought me here?"

"No, not yet. Makin says I'm not done yet. I was able to speak to my father, and he seems okay. But I don't know where they are." His voice trembles.

"I'm so sorry, Michael. But right now, I need some time and space to figure all this out," I answer coolly.

Michael slowly backs away, not looking at me. "I understand. I'll leave you alone. I'm sorry that all of this has happened to you." He pauses. "I...I know why your powers aren't working. I overheard Makin speaking with the Queen. An evil sorcerer has bound them, and they won't work until the binding spell is broken. I don't know who this sorcerer is, but when I find out, I'll tell you."

As quickly as Michael appeared, he is gone. He leaves me alone to ponder what he said. Who is this strong sorcerer that put a spell on me? Maybe Miri would know.

I stand there, not wanting to move, not wanting to believe this is my life. All I want is to go to the dance with Michael and live a normal teenage life. To think less than a week ago, I was studying for a biology test and making plans for a school dance. Now I'm stuck in outer space, and I'm a pawn in an intergalactic conflict soon to be an all-out war.

Being summoned for dinner is a little different than Elena calling up the stairs to tell me the pizza has been delivered. There's a knock at the door, and when I open it, I find Gabe standing there with a sealed letter addressed to me, and a large, pastel-pink box.

"Thank you, Gabe." I take the letter from him and reach for the box.

"Princess, I will carry this in for you." Gabe walks though the door and says over his shoulder, "May I place it on the bed?"

I look up from the off-white envelope in my hands, wondering what all this fuss is for. "Yes, thank you, that would be fine."

Gabe returns and stands in the doorway. "Do you need anything before I leave, Princess?"

"No, I'm all set; thank you, Gabe." He quickly inclines his head, then disappears around the corner.

I can't wait to see what the queen, my mother, is up to. I quickly open the envelope and am surprised to see an invitation:

Please join me in welcoming my daughter, Princess Alexis DeMarquis, to the island. Your attendance at tonight's honorary dinner is mandatory.
~ Your Queen

Great, just what I want to go to—a formal dinner with the queen and her people. Part of me is curious about who will show up. Will the elusive Council family members be there? Will Michael be there?

I glance over at the bed and remember the large, pink box waiting for me. "Hmmm, what could be in there?" My hands tremble as I lift the top off. A small green card sits perfectly on top of something protected within tissue paper. This time, the note is handwritten:

Alexa, I believe this dress will fit you perfectly.
~ Your Mother

I fold aside the tissue to unveil a stunning, silky-black gown scattered with glittering sequins. Gently, I lift it out of the box, in awe of its beauty.

Moving to the full-length mirror, I hold the dress up against my body. The sparkles are eye-catching. I've never in my life seen such a gorgeous gown. My purple eyes seem to glow against the midnight glamour of the dress.

I close my eyes and pretend to be home, enjoying a moment of happiness with Elena. I imagine her helping me get ready for my school dance. We would laugh and she'd lecture me about boys, but it would be memorable and heartwarming. Then guilt wells within me as I remember where I am and who I am. How can I put on a dress and attend a dinner when the ones I love are in danger because of who I am?

A knock on the door pulls me from my self-pity. I assume it's Miri, and that makes me happy. I slap on my best fake smile and open the door. "Miri, I'm so happy you came by. Are you attending the dinner tonight?" I move out of the doorway so she can slide in.

"Of course I am. Attendance is required of everyone on the island. I also hear that some are making the trip from the homeland just to see you." She flashes me a toothy grin and jumps on my bed.

"Coming to see *me*? Why?" I never liked being the center of attention, and this makes me feel I'm the feature at the circus tonight. This reminds me of my first and last attempt at dance. Elena made me commit to a summer of dancing and in the end I had to perform at a recital. It was horrible. Being the center of attention is my worst nightmare.

"Some beings have been waiting for you to return since your birth was first announced," Miri replies. "I think they're ready for a new face on the Council, since its members have dwindled over the years."

A sequin glints on the gown. It captures her attention, and Miri gasps and holds out her arms. I drape the dress over them. "That is gorgeous!" She studies the dress and then me. "Alexa, you'll be the talk of the evening in this stunning dress. Well, you're lovely now," she hastens to add, and giggles. "But this dress is just so pretty."

"Thanks," I say as I take it back from her. "It was sent from the queen." I try to appear happy, but the thoughts of Elena and my old life spiral around in my head.

Miri springs up off the bed. "Well, I just wanted to check in on you. Last time I saw you, Michael was insistent on speaking with you. Did that go well?"

I shrug. "I wouldn't say it went well. It's complicated. He lied, and I don't think I'll be able to forgive him or forget what he did. If he had been honest, then maybe I could." Michael's face comes to mind—his beautiful, big eyes and his soft lips that have left such a memorable impression. Why did I have to fall for him?

With a sigh, Miri walks to the bank of windows that overlook the beach. "That's too bad. Michael really is nice, and I do believe he cares about you. He's very protective of you, especially when you first arrived. He never left your side. You wouldn't know that, because you were unconscious."

The thought of Michael by my side does warm my heart, but it doesn't last long when I think of the big picture. "I need to focus on one thing at a time. Enough about Michael. Let's get ready for the dinner together."

Miri's face lights up. "You mean it? We can really get ready together?"

"Of course! Let's ask Gabe or Gavin to retrieve your dress. Then we can put on our makeup and do our hair." Miri's excitement is contagious; even I'm getting excited at the prospect.

Miri is still smiling, but she sobers just a bit to say sincerely, "Thank you, Alexa. I'm so happy we have each other now."

Her words bring some contentment to me, and for now, that will have to be enough. Tonight I need to see what Mother Dearest has planned for me, and who this sorcerer is. I'm ready to take control of my powers.

Sixteen

I TRY TO KEEP MY head down through dinner by focusing on both the delicious spread of food and Miri, who is sitting to my right. To my left sits Gabe and Gavin. Unfortunately, they have been by my side all evening. What am I, six years old again? This time I have two overbearing nannies. How am I supposed to sneak around and find a way out of this?

Behind our table sits my mother in the most beautiful, flowing, sea-green dress, along with the rest of the Council members. She sits in the middle with an elderly gentleman on each side of her. She hasn't introduced me to them yet, but I anticipate that time is coming.

In front of us, there are about twenty large round tables with twelve beings seated at each. I try not to stare, but I can't say the same for the guests. I can feel hundreds of eyes drilling holes through my body. Focusing on Miri helps because her laughter is infectious, but I can't quell an ominous feeling in the pit of my stomach.

"Miri, which way is the bathroom?" I murmur, and she gives me an awkward side glance, then motions toward a door with her hand.

"Through the door and to the left. Do you want me to come with you?"

I know she's just being nice. Plus, I'm a big girl and I can take myself to the bathroom alone. I smile and shake my head as I slowly push my seat back and rise. A sudden commotion of screeching chair legs in front of me makes me jump. Gazing out toward the audience, I'm shocked to see everyone standing, all staring at me. The disapproving glare from the queen behind me doesn't help, either.

Dumbfounded, I ask Miri, who is also standing. "What's happening?" I whisper.

Miri covers her mouth with one hand and whispers back, "Well, for starters, you're their princess, and it's customary to rise when royalty stands up." Miri grins bashfully and sits back down.

I nervously fumble past my chair and make a quick exit. I need air; I need to get out of here. Behind me, I can hear the chairs moving and the chatter resuming. I think it's safe to assume that dinner has continued.

I stand in the hallway for a minute, catching my breath, trying to process what just happened. This life is very different from the one I had been living. A familiar feeling flutters in the pit of my stomach and I gasp.

"Could it be—Jax?" I whisper to myself.

Jax can't possibly be here on this island. He is far away and only reachable from my dreamland. He has no idea where I am. It would be crazy to think that he could be here. Even so, the thought of his familiar face warms me. Although he took me from my home, I know that he cares about me. Why else would he be trying to find me?

"You're here to bring the water, are you not?" The woman startles me from my thoughts. She came out of nowhere. When I don't quickly respond, she grabs my arm and digs her nails into my flesh.

"Stop, that hurts!" I protest. Where are Gabe and Gavin when I need them? "I'm sorry. I don't know what you're talking about. I think you have me mistaken with someone else."

For an older woman, her grip is strong. Her gray hair is slicked up into a traditional bun on the top of her head. Her purple, chiffon dress fits snugly, accentuating her slight frame.

Her dark-gray eyes grow wider with my answer. I think she's expecting something else from me. "What do you mean, you don't know what I'm talking about? Why do you think you're here? Why do you think they have been searching for you for the past seventeen years?" She lets go of my arm and stands stiffly in front of me, waiting for an explanation, one that I don't have.

Out of the corner of my eye, I see Michael approaching. I sigh with relief.

"Good evening. Can I help you find your seat?" He holds out his bent arm for the woman to take.

"Please, and thank you. I was just paying my respects to the princess." The woman doesn't take her eyes off of me while she speaks to Michael.

Her unexpected outburst has left me confused. Water? I have no idea what she was talking about. This will be something else to ask Miri about when this charade of a dinner is over. I return my attention to the hall, where my mother the queen now mingles with the citizens of the island, who are all standing. She catches my eye and gives me a disapproving scowl.

I move in her direction, trying to soften the disaster I seem to have created. I flash her my best fake smile and she responds with a forced half-smile of her own. I don't know what's more confusing, the fact that I'm here attending my own welcome princess party, or the faint desire to please my mother. Both thoughts demand way too much energy, and that's something I need to conserve in order to find the truth.

"Princess." She glides toward me, extending her arm. "I take it you're settling in well here?"

"Yes, thank you." My half curtsy is as embarrassing as me ducking out during dinner. I really have no idea what I'm doing.

"I want you to meet two dear, dear friends and fellow Council members." She guides me around so I'm facing the two men who had been flanking her at dinner. "This is Penn Roberts and Eroch Finch. Gentlemen, this is my beautiful, gifted daughter, Alexa." Both gentlemen bow toward me.

As graciously as possible, I smile. "It's a pleasure to meet you." *Gifted daughter* repeats in my head. What does that mean?

The man introduced as Penn Roberts won't take his emerald-green eyes off of me. His gray locks look snarled and greasy, but I try not to stare, afraid my mother will catch me. Even though I'm not used to the customs here, it's safe to assume that staring is in bad form, no matter what planet you're on.

Eroch stands there idly waiting for something to happen. The awkward moment seems to last forever before my mother saves us all from the deafening silence.

"Princess, it's time we introduce you to your people." The queen smiles and wraps her arm around my shoulders. "I've been waiting all of your life for this day." Her words ring warm and sincere, but I keep replaying in my head all of the horrible things she's supposedly done: the rumored massacres, holding Michael's family hostage, binding my so-called magic, and taking Miri away from her mother—that's unforgivable.

"Queen, you are too kind." My eyes meet hers and I can tell she's thinking something, but she says nothing. She draws me back into the dinner room and escorts me around to her people and I struggle to remember what a bad queen and mother she is. However, every time we approach a new table, she says something so touching about me, recalling my birth into the world, or the legacy she's planned for me. How can she be so terrible and so kind all at the same time? These thoughts make my head spin.

"Princess, are you okay?"

The queen's words halt the whirling in my head. "Yes, Your Majesty. I'm just finding this evening both overwhelming and enlightening. I think it's all catching up to me." I smile with my reply.

"You'll be fine. After tonight, you can rest as long as you need to," she whispers in my ear. She grips my arm to steady me. The spinning starts to subside and I carry on as she expects me to.

I have to admit, meeting the people of Mapu went a lot more smoothly than I had originally imagined. The queen introduced me formally with a toast with a bubbly drink that fizzed in my mouth and warmed my stomach. The drink reminded me of Earth's champagne in both appearance and effect, I imagine, as well.

After the toast, Mother and I greet each table. With each introduction, my heart softens. I receive praise and comments riddled with relief that I'm finally here. Everyone is pleased and excited to meet me. Why would they display such pleasure if that's not the case? I find their happiness and sincerity touching, and I wonder if perhaps this is where I truly belong. Maybe this woman, my mother, the queen, isn't so bad?

Walking back to my room, I pause and remove my sparkling, magenta, open-toe heels and let my feet breathe. Miri didn't stay for much of the party after dinner. She was exhausted and Michael escorted her to her room as soon as dinner was over. She did say that she didn't sleep well the night before and she needed to rest. Thankfully, Mother was okay with that.

Since Gabe and Gavin are helping to escort the crowd out of the castle, I'm free to roam around on my own. However, all I can think about is my bed. Entertaining is surprisingly exhausting. Especially when trying not to upset my mother.

Gazing over the balcony on the way back to my room, I notice the tide is going out. The air smells sweet and salty, tickling my nose, and when I close my eyes, I imagine Elena and I vacationing in Maine. The imagery brings me back to a happy place.

"Princess, are you all right?"

I don't need to open my eyes to know who is standing behind me. I sensed Michael nearing me a few minutes ago. "Did Miri get tucked into bed okay?" I turn around to look at him and notice something is different about him.

"Yes, she did," he murmurs. Then his brows furrow as if he wants to say something, but instead, his face shifts into concern.

"Michael, what's wrong?"

He leans forward and his voice becomes urgent. "I shouldn't be here, or be telling you this. She will kill my family if she finds out."

I can sense his fear, almost *feel* it. Shivers travel through my body, chilling me. The calmness of a few minutes ago is gone, replaced by heart-pounding anxiety. "Michael, could you be wrong about her? She seems so gracious, and she clearly cares for the beings on her planet. Maybe the one who kidnapped your family is that terrible Makin?"

"That's what she wants you to think, Alexa. She's not nice, or good, or anything that a queen should be. She plays a game—and she plays it well. Have you forgotten how you got here? Or the place she sent me to retrieve you? I've been living a lie for a year, watching you and reporting back," he says, his voice heavy with disgust. "I'm afraid she's put a spell on you. She has made you only see what she wants you to see."

Michael takes a step toward me, holding out his hands. "Alexa, I know you have no reason to trust me, but you need to when it comes to her. She's evil."

"Michael, I do believe you when you speak about her and tell me these things. But when you leave, I think about how nice she is, and that maybe there's a chance we could have a mother-daughter relationship. I don't know why I think this after what you've told me, and what we've been through." I feel as frustrated as the day I arrived.

He gently brushes a strand of hair from my face and tucks it behind my ear. "Alexa, I don't know what her plan is, but I know your magic is being suppressed by a sorcerer on the island. I also know your mother had a spell cast over you, probably by this sorcerer, that makes you think about her as a motherly figure—not as the monster she is. Somehow, it suppresses your anger toward her. Your mother has no magical abilities, but she keeps people close by who do. She uses them to do her dirty work. Honestly, that's why I think she keeps Miri here. If things don't work out with you, she'll abuse Miri's power to rule." Michael takes a deep breath and sighs loudly. I can see subtle signs of the old Michael returning.

"Why are you telling me all this? How do I know you aren't under a spell?" I question.

"Awhile ago, after my family was taken, I asked Miri to put a block on me so no spell could be cast over me, unless she willed it herself. She has very strong abilities," Michael muttered.

"I'm not sure what I can do. But I'm going to do something." My voice sounds stronger than I feel, but I know if I don't believe in myself, no one will. "Michael, somehow, we need to locate the being who is preventing me from learning and using my abilities. You should work on that. I think you could probably move about the island easier than I can." I think of my two bodyguards and the ruckus I would cause if I were caught venturing out of the castle. If Michael works on this, I can work on a plan of my own.

"Alexa, please believe me when I say that I'll make this better," he says earnestly. "I'll do anything you ask of me to prove that I do care about you." His eyes search mine, silently begging me to believe in him.

Before I can speak, he moves closer. My will fails me. I stand there, half of me not wanting to move, the other half wanting to run. When he kisses me, it's different from before. His lips are still soft and familiar, but the magic is absent.

He pulls back and shrugs. "Alexa, I love you, and I'll prove to you that I'm the same person you were falling for on Earth before all of this happened."

Tears collect in the corners of my eyes. Sadness ripples through my entire body. "Michael, we have to focus on what's happening right now. I can't do this." My face warms with embarrassment at my emotional reaction.

He nods, steps back, and starts down the hall.

The moisture in my eyes spills over. Trying to see through tear-filled eyes, I stumble into my room.

The sobbing begins as I throw myself onto the bed. My breath catches in my throat as I replay Michael's admission of his feelings for me. Emptiness fills my heart, darkening my soul. My feelings for Michael have changed. The obstacles and lies have altered everything. I bury my face in my pillow and cry for the old Alexa and Michael, the two who studied for their biology exam and exchanged witty banter.

Those two people are gone.

Everything has changed.

Seventeen

"ALEXA, ARE YOU THERE?"

His voice reverberates within me, dragging me out of my sleep. I find myself lying on a bed of green flowers in our field; silence surrounds me. I lie there staring up at the sky, waiting to hear his voice again.

"Alexa, I'm almost there. We are coming to rescue you. I'm not sure if you can hear me, but be ready."

"Jax, where are you? I can't see you." The tree line is looming before me. I wait to hear a response from Jax but the silence is maddening.

The three moons lined up in the sky above me begin to blink and darken in color. Once orange, they now glow more crimson. My body begins to quake. The moons are also growing in size. No! They aren't only growing, they're moving closer!

I spring to my feet, heart pounding, panic tightening my chest, preventing me from taking a deep breath. I stumble toward the forest, my bare feet sinking into the soggy grass, making a sucking noise each time I pick up my foot. I don't let that stop me.

When I make it to the tree line I gaze up and behind me to see if the moons are still plummeting toward me. Yes! The magenta light filtering though the trees begins to darken. I struggle to see what's right in front of me, but I keep moving, too afraid to stop.

My feet hurt, bruised from running over rocks, sticks, and other bits on the forest floor. I clench my teeth and run through the pain. A loud noise echoes behind me, and I know the sky is falling. All I can do is run. Sweat trickles down my face and a fire burns in my chest. I close my eyes and continue to run.

"Alexa, wake up!" Miri's hands shake my shoulders. "Please, wake up!" Her voice is loud, but at the same time, it sounds so far away.

"Miri?" My voice is barely audible. I blink and open my eyes to see two large, lilac eyes staring back at me. Worry sprawls across her face.

I slowly sit up and quickly notice that we aren't in my room. "Where are we?"

Miri puts a finger over her lips. "Shhhh, keep your voice down," she admonishes. "If we get caught, both of us will be in big trouble." Her usual carefree expression is very serious. "I came to check on you after the dinner because I couldn't stay asleep. When I got to your room, you were just leaving. I could tell you weren't awake, but you wouldn't stop when I called your name."

I lower my mouth to her ear. "So where are we? Where did I go?" Shivers spill down my back, making my whole body shudder.

Miri's pale face looks even whiter, if that's possible. "I followed you out of the castle and into the woods. I've never been out this far before, but you seemed as if you were on a mission, like you've been here before. We came to a little house in the woods and you walked right in."

"Well, why don't we just leave?" I'm perplexed. How is this an issue? Why would we get into trouble? But I know there must be more to the story.

"Before you woke up, I could hear two male voices outside the house. I recognized one as Makin, but I'm not sure who the other voice belongs to." Noticeably, Miri tenses up and tiny quivers run through her body. "They were shouting back and forth, something about your powers, and then the voice I didn't recognize screamed like he was in pain. And then the shouting stopped."

I look around, taking a better inventory of my surroundings. If a fight is going to erupt, I need to see what I can use to defend us. I slowly stand, hunched over, and creep over to crouch below the window and peer out. "Maybe Makin left," I whisper. "I don't see anyone. How long ago did this happen?"

"Maybe ten minutes ago." Miri pulls her knees up against her chest. "Why wouldn't you wake up? What were you dreaming about?" A single tear rolls down her cheek and falls to the wooden floorboards she's sitting on.

"I...I don't remember. All I know is that I was running from something." I close my eyes, trying to recall my dream. Where did I just come from? I could tell from the pounding of my heart against my ribcage that whatever I'd been dreaming about had really scared me.

"Miri, can you use your magic to see or sense who is outside this cabin?" I try to appear calm and in control. I don't want to upset Miri; she's my little sister and I'm protective. It's hard to explain, but keeping her safe is my top priority.

"Yes, let me try." Miri closes her eyes and sits very still.

A high-pitched ringing echoes around me, and I slap my hands over my ears, trying to muffle the piercing noise. Flashes of red and images of fire singe the back of my eyelids.

"Alexa, what's wrong?" Miri grabs my arm, but the noise is debilitating and I can't bear the idea of moving my hands away from my head. The pain brings tears to my eyes. They flow down my face and dampen the floor.

"You're bleeding. Alexa, what do I do? Your ears are bleeding!"

My own screaming drowns Miri's frantic pleas out. I blink open my eyes and I can only see darkness. Miri's hands are on my arm and squeezing me tightly, but I can't hear her or see her.

Panic clutches at my chest and fear paralyzes my whole body. I know it's only a matter of time before I pass out. But I want to hold on. I want to be there for my sister!

"Alexa, listen to me!" The man's voice is louder than the piercing ringing, louder than my shrieks. "Take a deep breath."

His voice is soothing and I focus on it. I focus on my breathing and count. One, two, three, four, five—I blink my eyes open, but I still can't see anything.

"Miri, where are you?" My voice comes labored and echoing. It sends a stabbing pain into my head.

"Alexa, don't speak. You need to rest. Miri is right here, safe. You're both safe." The man's voice is lulling me into a restful state. He gently rubs my arm and I instantly find comfort.

Thoughts flicker around in my head. I don't fight it or even try to talk; for some reason, I trust this unknown voice. "That's it, Alexa, don't panic. There will be plenty of time to talk." His voice trails off and my body relaxes.

Jax is standing over me as I begin to open my eyes. His muscles ripple through his tight-fitting, long-sleeved, white shirt. I find myself admiring him, wondering if he knows why I'm goofily staring at him. "I must be dreaming..."

"Don't seem so excited, Alexa." He purses his pouty lips, then offers me a weak smile. "You're not dreaming; we rescued you."

I slowly sit up, noticing I'm in yet another room that I don't recognize. There's a dull throb in the back of my head, so I don't move my head too quickly.

Before I can ask any questions, he hands me a glass of water and a peanut butter and jelly sandwich. The smell of the peanut butter instantly makes my mouth water. "I thought you might be hungry; you haven't eaten in a few days."

I practically launch the sandwich into my mouth. "I can still ask questions," I say around a mouthful, then quickly chew and swallow. "So, am I dreaming, or did you kidnap me from yet another place?" I flash him a smile, letting him know that either way, I'm happy he's here.

His blue eyes are dark, deep pools that I can't look away from. "I prefer rescue. When we got to you, you were in quite a state." His playful expression turns grim. He motions for me to move my legs so he can sit down next to me. "Do you remember what happened?"

"You're making me nervous, Jax. Why are you being so serious?"

"You don't remember?" He moves closer. I can feel his breath on my neck, and a warm sensation surges through me. "I was so scared, Alexa. I thought I was going to lose you."

I tilt my head and slide back on the bed, putting a bit of distance between us. "Um, I remember being in a cabin with Miri—oh, my god, Miri! Where is she? Is she okay?"

I throw the remaining bite of my sandwich to the ground and jump up from the bed only to be seized by Jax. His strong arms wrap around me, holding me still. A tingling sensation travels through me and sparks begin to ignite where he touches me. I shake myself free of him and sit back down. What was that?

"Miri is fine. You can see her soon. When we got to the cabin, you were having a seizure. It was pretty serious. It has something to do with your magic. We believe someone tried casting a spell on you using your own magic. We aren't sure who did it, but we were able to stop it." The corners of his mouth rise, revealing a toothy grin. "We're just so happy you're better. It's been three days since the cabin, and Miri is driving me crazy!"

"Three days! It feels like it has only been three minutes." I try and remember what I saw last. "I can't believe I've been unconscious for three whole days. We? What do you mean, 'we'?" I spit out.

On cue, the door creaks open and a tall man walks in. His light-brown hair and familiar eyes make me ill. "Mr. Riley?" I exclaim. "You're the 'we'? I don't get it."

As soon as he begins talking, I instantly remember the last moments I had in the cabin. He's the man with the soothing voice. I close my eyes in disbelief and pull up my memories from school with Mr. Riley. He's a biology teacher—and a strange one, at that. Why would he be here?

"Alexa, please, you need to calm down. You had us all really worried."

I hesitate, then blurt, "So I was not only fooled by Michael, but by my biology teacher, as well." Wow, so much for being astute and aware of the behavior of the people around you.

"Well, it's not like that. I was there to watch over you and ensure your safety." He darts his eyes around the room, avoiding my gaze.

"So go on, then," I quickly counter.

Uncomfortable, Mr. Riley clears his throat. "Well, I didn't want to tell you like this, but here it goes. My real name is Kalus. It just so happens that I'm your father."

My back stiffens and I fight the urge to vomit. I look over at Jax to see his cool-blue eyes studying me, waiting for my blowout reaction or complete breakdown. "You've got to be joking!" I yell, unable to suppress my shock.

"Did you know this?" I shoot Jax a glare.

"I just found out a few days ago," he answers solemnly.

Kalus, from what I've heard, is the most strategically gifted warrior in the galaxy. How can this same being be Mr. Riley? This is the being that left me with Elena and fabricated my whole entire life up to this point!

The emotions running through me are a jumble of excitement, resentment, and relief. The fact that he isn't dead, as I was told on several separate occasions, is not only shocking, but also favorable...I think. Maybe now I can get some honest answers and find out what else about my life is a lie.

"Say something, Alexa. Scream at me, hit me, say something." Mr. Riley continues to stare at me, waiting for me to erupt.

I roll my eyes. "What I need is some answers. Where are we? Where is the queen, and what happened to my powers?"

A smirk crawls across Jax's face. "Well, I can brief you there, but first, let's get you out of here and find Miri. She'll be so mad that I didn't tell her the moment you woke up."

"Fine." I leap up, concerned with how Miri is taking the news. "Let's find her."

"Wait, Alexa, I owe you some sort of explanation. I need to tell you what happened. The reason I left you with Elena." His eyebrows wrinkle and grief plays across his face.

Tears gather in my eyes, but crying isn't an option. "I don't have anything to say to you right now. I just want to talk to my sister. Did you tell her? Does she know who you are?"

He pauses and I try to imagine what he's thinking. Is this weird for him, too? "I didn't have to tell her. She witnessed me trying to help you. She said, 'It would make sense that only our father could make you better, because he has the strongest magic.'"

A smile spreads across my face. That sounds just like her. Miri is exceptionally attentive to detail. I'm so happy to have found her. Right now, I can only think of her and what our future looks like.

"Is that true? Is your magic the strongest?" I wonder aloud. If this is true, then maybe I can get my magic back and figure out how to fix what my mother and Makin broke.

Mr. Riley—Kalus—my father—hesitates. "It could be, but I haven't practiced my abilities since the day I left you, fourteen years ago."

I ponder that statement for a minute. "Why?"

"If I practiced magic, they would have been able to find me. I was always close by, and if they found me, they inevitably would have found you." He takes a deep breath and lets it out slowly. "Oh, I wanted to keep you with me, while refraining from my magic, but I couldn't take the chance. I love you too much, Alexa. It was best to have you safe with Elena instead of even that shred of danger with me."

"What about Miri? Why didn't you rescue her from the queen?"

His face flushes red and his jaw tenses. "I didn't know she existed until just recently." Pain weights his words. "Her mother and I met on Earth thirteen years ago, and within a few months of our courtship, she was summoned back to Mapu. She had no way to tell me, and she feared if she reached out, they would find me—or even worse, that they would find you."

"I don't get it—why would she care if they found me?" I demand, growing angry. "How dare she leave Miri with that woman?"

"You don't know, do you? She didn't tell you." His red face quickly drains of blood, until it's pale, almost ashen.

"Tell me what?" I ask. "What am I missing?"

"You, my dear, are the key. Once your magic is restored, you'll have the ability to rule not only Pumalia and Mapu, but the whole galaxy," he confesses. "You are the sole hope for all of our futures. The queen only held Miri for her powers, to see what they evolve into."

I swallow a sudden lump in my throat. The room whirls around me. "There has to be a mistake," I sputter.

"I'm afraid not," he answers. "You and your powers have been prophesied for hundreds of years. The beings of this galaxy have been waiting for you."

I feel myself swaying. Jax appears by my side. "Alexa, don't pass out. Just breathe, in and out." I lean against him while I focus on not blacking out.

The idea that I could do anything so remarkable is beyond me. This guy, Kalus, or Mr. Riley, or whoever he is, he's nuts.

A child's voice breaks the tension. "Alexa, I'm so happy you're awake!" Miri bounds over to me with her arms wide open. She hugs me and her touch instantly calms me.

"Do you believe him, Miri?" I ask. "Is this all true? Do you know what he's saying?"

She giggles, as usual. "I knew who you were and what you were destined to do before I even met you. Everyone knows, but I knew you weren't ready to hear it."

I step back. "You knew?"

Jax throws up his hands in defense. "I did not know, for the record," he confesses. "I mean, I knew you were different, but I didn't know you were The One that the oracle spoke of."

"Oracle?" I question.

Miri lets out an exaggerated laugh. "Our dad has a lot of explaining to do." She reaches out and takes my hand in hers. "Let's get some fresh air."

I let Miri lead me out of the room, through an adjoining room, and outside. As soon as we step out, I know exactly where we are. We're in hiding. I'm back underground in Aurora.

Eighteen

MIRI AND I WALK AROUND Aurora. I point out a few places I know and take her toward the woods, where I escaped from before. Like me, she's in awe that such a place exists underground. Every time a being walks by, she stares directly at them and smiles or waves. The beings always smile back, and a few return the wave. She's so kind and worldly at such a young age.

"Well, well, Alexa is back," a familiar voice snarls behind me. I know instantly that it's Tam.

I turn around to catch her rolling her eyes in my direction. "Um, hi, Tam," I reply. The tension between us is obvious. "This is Miri, my sister." I watch Tam's expression soften as soon as she glances over and spies Miri. Maybe she isn't as rude as I remember.

"So, what brings you back here? Endangering all of us here wasn't enough for you? You bring your boyfriend here, who works for the queen, and now they know where we are. Aurora is in danger because of you," she snaps at me.

Her words sting. I would never want to cause anyone harm. "It's not like that. I didn't bring Michael here. He found me, and he made me believe him. I trusted that if I went with him, I would protect the people here and find the answers I was seeking. I never meant to hurt you or Kasper, or anyone, for that matter."

"Well, you did," she barks. "Some beings are terrified that she, your mother, is going to come here and kill us all."

Miri squeezes my hand and says, "Don't worry, Tam, our father will protect everyone here, I promise!"

Before Tam walks away, she gives Miri a half-smile and says, "I hope you're right."

Jax comes up behind me and puts his hands on my shoulders. His mere touch is all the comfort I need right now. "She'll come around. She's just upset and scared for everyone here in Aurora."

"I can't believe I have endangered all of these beings," I whisper. "What have I done?"

"Stop," he says, turning me to face him. "Alexa, it's not your fault. The queen knows this place exists. She just didn't know how to sneak in here until recently when Michael was able to breach the barrier. She had help, and that's not on you. The being that gave Michael access to this place is to blame. Not you, do you understand?" The tone of Jax's voice scares me. He's angry, and it only makes me feel worse.

"But he came for me. It's my fault," I lament. He gently pulls me into a strong embrace. "What are we going to do?" I sob into his chest.

"We fix it," he replies in a low voice. I let him hold me a moment longer. His touch is warm, and in his arms, I'm safe.

"Are you two done?" Kasper's voice peels me off of Jax sooner than I wished.

"Hi, Kasper, are you here to yell at me, too?"

I'm surprised to see Kasper trying to keep a straight face. "I take it you ran into Tam?" He laughs at my expense, as usual.

"You think it's funny that she basically blames me for a possible attack on Aurora?" I ask. "You think it's funny that on top of all of these revelations, I now have to worry about my mother coming for me here?"

Kasper doesn't wipe his smirk off his face. Instead, he replies, "Alexa, you didn't know this would happen, did you? I don't want to burst your bubble, but it's not your fault."

"Okay, so what's the plan to keep this place protected?" I ask, wanting to know just how this problem will be remedied.

"Don't you know who your father *is*, Alexa? We don't have to worry, he has it covered." Kasper is now acting annoyed and less smug. "You need to work on your powers, you know, like we started here before."

"Okay, go easy on her, Kasper. She's been through a lot," Jax barks in my defense.

"We don't have time to hold her hand and walk her through this process. We tried that. It didn't work," Kasper retorts.

Jax throws up his hands. "Well, you can place that blame on me, as well, for not being straightforward from the beginning."

Miri pipes in and silences both of them. "No one here is to blame. There have been a lot of lies, and it's been hard for Alexa to distinguish what's true and what's not. How would she know who to trust, even if Jax told her up front what was happening?" Miri sighs. "Unfortunately, these things have happened, and we all need to move forward."

Jax and Kasper nod in agreement. Sometimes, I find it hard to believe that Miri is only twelve years old. She's wise beyond her years.

"I'm sorry if you think Tam and I come off harsh. We really just want to help you out. We still do, if you want us to," Kasper comments.

"Sure, that would be great," I say, though I don't know if I actually feel that way. "You do know my powers are gone though, right?"

Kasper grins. "They aren't gone, they're suspended, but we're already working on that. Why don't you three meet me in the center of town right before sundown? We will explain then."

I'm not sure why, but I search Jax's eyes for some sort of approval. He nods and I take that as a yes. "Okay. We'll be there. Thanks again for giving me another chance, Kasper. I promise I won't let everyone down again."

"I know you won't," Kasper responds as he walks away.

"Alexa, you need to go easy on yourself," Jax says gravely. "You can't keep beating yourself up for what's happened."

"He's right, Alexa. It's time to focus on what lies ahead, not what you left behind." Miri smiles and wraps her arms around me.

I rest my head on her shoulder and squeeze her tight. "I love having a wise younger sister," I whisper. "Are you hungry? Let's go get something to eat."

Miri nods. "Jax, do you want to come with us?"

"Thanks for the offer, but I'm meeting your father for a tactical walk-through of the perimeter. I'll join you two in town this evening." He pats my shoulder and walks off. The tingling sensation from his touch travels down my arm and I can't help but smile.

"You like him, don't you?" Miri notes right away. Her observation, even though naive, makes me wonder if Jax and I indeed have some sort of connection. A connection would explain why I experience sparks every time he brushes up against me.

"No, it's not like that," I stammer, giving myself away. We both laugh. "Come, little sister, let's go find something to eat."

After lunch, I continue to show Miri around Aurora. She, too, can't believe the incredible, sustainable life that these beings have made available for themselves down here. It almost seems an impossible feat.

"Do you think they miss being with their families on their own planets?" Innocently, she glances up at me, blinking her big, oval eyes.

"I do think they miss both their families and their planet. It's odd, even though I don't belong on Earth, I still long for the normalcy of it. Especially after being thrown into this mess." I smirk, knowing that living on Earth would never be enough now. "But losing Earth has all been worth it since I now have a smart, beautiful, brave little sister."

We both giggle and continue back toward Kasper's house. In a few hours, we will be addressing the beings that live down here, but until then, I need to make sure Miri and I get some rest.

"Wait up, you two!" My heart quickens when I hear Jax running up behind us.

I angle around to see Jax approaching. He has a handsome grin plastered on his typically stoic face.

"What can we do for you?" I ask spiritedly.

"Actually, I was hoping to talk to you alone for a minute, Alexa, if that's okay with you?" A surge of red color creeps onto his face. Is Jax blushing?

"Sure. Miri, I'll meet you back at Kasper's place in a short while. Make sure you lay down and rest."

"Yes, I'm tired. Take your time, I'll see you in a bit." Miri flashes me a toothy grin and I know what she's thinking. She quickly spins around and continues toward Kasper's.

"So are you going to attempt to kidnap me again?" I try to lighten the mood, but when I jokingly glance over at Jax, he looks pretty upset.

"Actually, that's what I want to talk to you about. I can't help but feel totally responsible for everything that's happened. If I had tried harder to figure out why your case was so different, or why Maddox seemed to fear you, then I think a lot of this could have been avoided."

We both continue to walk toward the waterfall in a comfortable silence. I'm not sure what to say or even how I feel about his confession.

I draw in sweet air and let it out. "I do think there was a better way to do everything. However, I don't hold you responsible for everything that's happened. How were you supposed to know just how in the dark I was, and how clueless I was about everything?" Flashes of Michael make me feel ill—how could I let him pretend to love me?

"If I had only done things differently, you wouldn't be so hurt," he sighs. "Michael wouldn't have gotten that close to you, and you wouldn't feel responsible for letting him into your life."

I abruptly stop walking and face Jax. "Listen, it's my own fault for falling for Michael and believing his nonsense. That's on me, not you."

Jax's serious expression returns to his face. "So you did fall for him?"

The question completely catches me off guard. Why would Jax care one way or the other?

"I don't know. I definitely cared for him, and a few times I even pictured myself with him. All that's changed now." Most of the time I continued to daydream about Jax, even when I was comfortably with Michael. I wonder if I should tell him that, too?

Jax clears his throat and adds, "Oh, well I'm sorry things didn't work out." We continue walking toward the waterfall.

"I'm not. It's better to know now instead of believing something that isn't real. I'd like to believe that he's not all bad, and the situation is just the result of my mother's mayhem."

We sit on the rock overlooking the pool of water. Even though we're both quiet, it's comfortable and it's like I'm sitting with an old friend.

"Jax, how is it possible that we can communicate still, even though I'm no longer on Earth being transitioned?"

"That's a great question, Alexa. I've also been wondering the same thing. I mentioned it to Kalus and he has never heard of anything like this. I think it's best we keep it between the three of us. I would hate for the wrong person to find out and exploit this—our special way of communicating, I mean."

"I agree." I rest my head on Jax's shoulder and close my eyes. A tingling sensation streams from my face into my whole body. The feeling is warm and comforting, and I wonder if Jax feels it, too.

"Alexa, we should go. Even though I could spend the whole day right here with you, we have a big night tonight."

Disappointment courses through me, but I know he's right. "Okay, since you put it like that, let's go. But this is your last chance to kidnap me. I'm alone, and no one would ever know." I start to laugh, but Jax just stares goofily at me.

"Well, there's one thing I want to do." Before I know what's happening, he has my face cradled in his hands and his lips are brushing up against mine. His plump lips fit perfectly on mine. My whole body becomes listless as I steady myself against him, all while his warm breath tickles my face.

Jax slowly separates, and the tingling, warm sensation leaves with him. That ended too soon. I want more. I need more.

"Are you mad at me?" he asks.

I nod. I can't form words for a few moments. I suck in a gulp of air and gaze into his beautiful eyes. "Yes, why did you stop?"

We both smile.

Jax is the first one to stand up. I still feel wobbly, and I think he knows it. He grabs my hands and guides me toward him.

"Alexa, we can take this slow. I want to be with you, but I'll wait until you're ready."

The admission catches me by surprise, and I'm lacking a response. Instead, I let it soak in and I think about what he has said. He'll wait for me. That's the kindest thing anyone has ever revealed to me.

I reach for his hand and give it a tight squeeze. I don't let go the whole walk back from the waterfall. I just enjoy it for what it is.

Nineteen

STANDING IN THE CENTER of Aurora, I watch as the beings that live here congregate. "I guess Kasper invited everyone," I whisper to Miri.

"I think the announcement affects everyone, and it's easier to get the word out when everyone is present," she answers.

She always does that; she makes everything sound positive. I, on the other hand, instantly think he invited them all here to see me, the one who led their enemy to their hiding place. Fear pulses through me. Part of me is nervous to hear the wrath of this eclectic bunch, and an even larger part of me is afraid to actually see all of the beings in one place.

"Miri, are you nervous about seeing all the different aliens?" I whisper in her ear.

"Nervous?" She quickly hides her face behind her hand. She's giggling so hard, I think she may start to cry. "Why would I be nervous? We are all aliens, we are all different—why would that make you nervous?"

There's nowhere to hide, and all I want to do is sink into the ground. My face is hot with embarrassment. I know it must be flaming red. "Kasper told me not to stare at them directly in their eyes because they get mad. He told me they would attack."

Miri stifles her laughter when she realizes I'm serious. "Don't you think Kasper is just saying that to you so you won't obnoxiously stare?" she asks quietly. "I don't believe any being here wants to cause anyone harm. Just because someone may appear different than you, that doesn't mean they want to attack you."

Her confidence makes me feel better. If she isn't nervous, then there's no reason for me to be.

Out of the corner of my eye I see my father, or Mr. Riley, walking toward us. Part of me wants to run and hide, but I know I can't leave. Instead, I take a few deep breaths, trying to calm myself.

"How are you two doing?" he asks when he joins us, taking time to touch on each of us with his penetrating gaze.

"Um, I'm okay," I answer.

"I'm good, Dad. How's the tactical surveillance going?"

I blink at her. How can she so easily call him Dad, after everything we've been through? I avert my eyes, then study my surroundings, trying to seem uninterested in their father-daughter conversation. I pretend to be interested in the six windowless, cement towers that surround the center of Aurora, and vaguely wonder what they represent.

"Alexa, are you okay?"

My father decides this is the time to ask me if I'm okay? I mean, really—in front of all these people, he wants to have this conversation? "Sure. I'm fine. How are you, Dad?" I mumble.

"Alexa, I know you're cross with me, but we need to work together. There's a lot we need to talk about before we leave here." His light-brown eyes are changing as he speaks to me, dark-blue and purple hues swirling around his irises. He's changing right in front of me. That means I must be, too, and if I am, then all of the other gathering beings are, as well.

"Um, yeah, we will," I answer quickly.

Miri senses my uneasiness and reaches for my hand. She gives it a tight squeeze, reassuring me that everything is going to be fine. I had forgotten while I was away from Pumalia that upon my return, some of my features might change; as Michael told me before, the camouflage wears off more or less when you're around your true heritage.

Standing on tiptoe, Miri whispers in my ear, "Your eyes are gorgeous! They're even more magical here than they were on Mapu. The purple has changed into a violet with blue accents—just beautiful."

"Yours, too, Miri," I respond, gazing into her eyes. "They're now darker, like Dad's." His eyes went from a green on Earth to a deep, deep blue. This revelation makes her happy, and if she's happy, then I am, too.

I smile and let that sink in. I guess it's true—you can't help where you're from or what your appearance is. I need to embrace it and move on.

The light starts to dim and I can sense the changes happening in the crowd of beings. I'm not scared anymore; instead, I'm intrigued.

Before I can actively search for the more alien-looking creatures that I've always imagined living in outer space, Kasper saunters up onto a small wooden stage and calls for everyone's attention. Wearing a black jacket to match his jet-black hair, and what seem to be jeans, Kasper stands confidently in front of the crowd. His lanky body is taller than I remember, and his pale skin is now a translucent mauve. This is his true form. I never even asked what planet he's from. I just assumed he was from Pumalia.

"Thank you all for coming tonight," he begins. "I know this isn't easy for anyone. But—the time is here. The time when we fight to win back our freedom. No longer will we cower from the Council or bow before the so-called queen."

The crowd erupts with shouts and affirmations that he's indeed on the right track. He waits for the noise to quiet before he continues. "We now have help with this matter. Not just any help, but the help that was prophesied to us thousands of years ago."

I stand very still, bracing myself for what's to come next. A tall, dark figure emerges from behind Kasper and approaches the front of the stage—Jax. The sight of him takes my breath away, and memories from the rock make my face blush. Good thing it's dark out. His blue eyes are glowing—not in a creepy way; they're mesmerizing. I can't look away.

"Thank you for meeting with us this evening," he says, his voice carrying over the crowd. "For those of you who don't know me, my name is Jax, and I have been the militia leader of Pumalia for the past seven years." His voice weakens my knees.

"Like Kasper, I feel this is the time to reclaim our lives and stand up for what's ours. No more living in fear of what the Council may do next. Pumalia is an independent sovereignty, but the decisions made are a direct result of what will make Mapu happy. I now realize that mentality will not work. Unfortunately, the people I serve don't see it that way." He sighs heavily. "That means we will be doing this ourselves."

The crowd clearly doesn't like that last statement, but Jax rebounds with, "Did I say by ourselves? I meant to say we will have to do this with the most decorated militia leader in the galaxy! Please welcome my hero and our savior, Kalus."

The beings go crazy at the very mention of him, hollering and chanting his name. My heart pounds as I watch my father approach the stage. Why are they reacting like this? Why am I nervous for him? The emotions churn in my stomach, making me nauseous.

"Miri, how do all of these beings know who he is?" I ask, dumbfounded.

Miri proudly smiles and replies, "He's a legend. He has fought many battles and his side always wins. They attribute much of those wins to one person, Kalus.

"Please, that's enough." He raises his arms in an effort to calm their excitement. "We have our work cut out for us, but I'm confident we will succeed. We will work together and take care of one another. Here in Aurora, this is our family and we will fight for one another until we're all free to live how and where we want."

Miri attentively listens and I watch as a single tear falls from her eye. She holds herself proud yet she wears an expression of fright. Sometimes I think this is too much for someone her age. But time and time again, she proves to be wise beyond her years.

"I want to introduce the being that you have all been buzzing about. This young woman is my daughter. I'm proud to call her that; she's strong and kind. She's the Princess of the Galaxy, and I know, not because I'm her father or because she's honorable, but I know she'll do everything in her power to restore its legacy."

All eyes turn in my direction. I can't believe this is happening to me. I'm going to kill him.

"Alexa, please join me up here."

I stand there dumbstruck for a moment, unable to move. I picture myself walking up there, but my legs are firmly planted in the ground beneath me.

Thankfully, Miri grabs my arm and pulls me toward the stage. Jax reaches for my hand and helps me up. I stand up there next to my father while everyone before us kneels down on one knee.

I can't believe what I see. There are beings of all colors and sizes. Some have more than one head, while others have tiny heads and no arms. The differences between the beings are immense, but they all kneel as one. They believe in me. They need me.

The gesture is inspirational; it gives me the strength I need to address them. "Please get up, I haven't done anything worthy of you kneeling down in front of me yet. But please believe me when I say I'll do whatever I can to right the wrongs of the queen and her followers." I look over at my sister and she gives me the biggest smile I've ever seen. I can't add anything else because the crowd is wildly cheering.

As Kasper and Jax try to restore order, my father ushers me off the stage, I assume for safety purposes. "Find your sister and get back to the house. I'm going to help them get everyone settled," Kalus says quickly.

"Okay," I say, and he marches back toward the cheering crowd. Just like that, I'm doing what he tells me. Am I already conforming to the father-daughter relationship? I quickly find Miri on the edge of the mayhem. We're able to sneak off before anyone can engage us in conversation, and head back to the house.

I tuck Miri into bed, which I assume will become a nightly duty that I not only enjoy, but also look forward to. Her sweet disposition is a welcomed distraction in this whole mess.

"Alexa, you're the most beautiful princess I've ever seen," she whispers as I pull the covers up to her chin.

"Aw, that's so sweet of you to say, Miri, but I don't feel much like a princess at the moment. There's so much to do, and I don't want to mess up," I confess.

She looks up at me with her beautiful lilac eyes. "It will come naturally, just like using your powers, I promise." She sounds so confident, it's hard to doubt her.

"Enough about me. How are you doing with all of the changes? Meeting our father for the first time—I can't be the only one having a hard time with it," I admit.

"I've dreamt of meeting him so many times. For me it was never a matter of if I'd meet him, but when." She briefly smiles at me, then flips onto her side. "I love you, Alexa. I'm so happy we found each other." Her voice now a whisper, while she grows more and more tired with each passing second.

"I love you, too, little sister." I bend over and kiss her cheek. "Good night, sweet girl."

I step out of the room and find a comfortable place on the couch to sit and reflect on the strange evening.

My father is a well-known leader and honored by every being here. Maybe I was being too hard on him? I really need to spend some time with him and hear more about what happened to me when I was a young child.

I close my eyes and attempt to center myself. A breeze wafts in through the open window and ruffles my hair. Simultaneously my emotions swirl around in my head, leaving me confused. But as exhaustion begins to settle in, my state of confusion fades.

Jax's face enters my thoughts and my whole body relaxes. His blue eyes and chiseled body make me blush even in my relaxed state. When he holds me, I know I'm safe. Maybe I do have feelings for him. Miri could be on to something.

"Alexa!"

I open my eyes to complete chaos. Jax is standing over me, yelling something, but I can't hear anything he's saying. A loud, piercing ring is obstructing his voice. Not again, I think. "What's happening?" I scream. Warm liquid trickles from my ears. I don't need to touch it with my hand to confirm it's blood.

Clenching my hands to my ears, I watch the beings in the house shuffle about, screaming. I can't tell what they're saying. For a minute, I stand there staring at them like an idiot as they dash around me. What could they possibly be searching for? Why don't they care about my ears? I'm bleeding!

I squint, hoping to clear the fuzziness hindering my vision, but it doesn't work. Somehow, I'm able to make out who's around me: Kasper, Tam, and another being whom I've never seen before.

I zone in on Miri's room in time to see Jax and my father storm out. My heart begins to pound. Where is she? I wish I could hear what they're saying! Tears sting my eyes. "Wait! What's happening?" I shout.

No one hears me; no one even acknowledges me. I push past the beings and enter Miri's room. She isn't there. Her bedding is a mess of sheets wound with her blanket, not how I left them when I tucked her in. Where could she be? I'd just left her. I only fell asleep for a few moments.

I dash back into the other room, where everyone has gathered in front of the couch. Why are they standing there? I finally give in and peer at the couch and I see—me. How can this be?

My stomach drops and a warm sensation slides up the back of my throat. The ringing is subsiding, but I can't breathe. I stumble to the door to get some air, feeling as if I'm being strangled by warm cotton batting stuffed into my airway.

Deep breaths, in and out, I admonish myself, breathing deeply and slowly. I close my eyes and imagine I'm home on Earth in my bed, and this is all a terrible dream. I must be dreaming—I have to believe that. Darkness engulfs me, along with a sense of overwhelming hopelessness. Where is she? I sink to the ground and lie curled up, letting everything fade around me.

Just as I shut my eyes, I'm opening them. I wake to the hum of low voices. The ringing is gone. I try to move my head to the right to see who's there, but my head is too heavy to control. Groaning aloud, I move my arms to get some attention.

"She's awake," I hear Tam say.

"Get Jax, he'll know how to tell her," Kasper solemnly requests.

I blink repeatedly, trying to rid my eyes of the fog that still clouds my sight. I'm dreaming, that's all; I probably slept too long. I'm sure Miri is up and making friends as I lie here in a stupor.

I can sense Jax before I see him. Just as I did in my dreams, when I always knew when he was in the field or on his way. He kneels down beside me and grabs my hand. "Are you okay?"

My mouth is so dry, my lips stick together. I can barely pry open my mouth to reply softly, "I think so. What happened? I had a terrible dream... Where's Miri?"

Jax doesn't have to say anything. I can tell by his expression that I wasn't dreaming.

"No, no, no!" I screech. "Is it true, is she gone?" Tears fall from my face as I lift my head. "Not my sister, *no!*"

"I'm so sorry, Alexa," Jax says. "When we came back after the gathering, you were under a spell. And...and she was gone."

Black spots flash in front of my eyes. The last thing I remember hearing is my own bloodcurdling screams before darkness takes over.

Coming soon!

DISORDER

Book 2 of the Stellar Series

THERE ARE NO WORDS. How could this have happened, right in front of me? "Could she still be here, in Aurora?" I scream loud enough for the whole room to hear me. As soon as the words leave my mouth, I know the answer. She's gone. Undoubtedly, this has something to do with my mother. Why did I ever think she wasn't culpable of such terror? It must have been the spell that prevented me from seeing her true colors.

"Possibly, but I doubt it." Jax wearily searches the room looking for someone. Before I can follow his glance, Michael appears next to me, refusing to look me in the eyes, which is fine. The mere sight of him makes my skin crawl. Obviously, he has something to do with taking my sister.

"I can't believe after everything that's happened, you have the gall to show up here," I angrily growl. "Did you take her? Was this your plan?" My fists clench so tightly that I'm sure I've cut myself. As I glare into his once-appealing brown eyes, I'm acutely aware that this isn't the same boy. The one I was developing feelings for.

"No, I could never hurt Miri. I love her like a little sister. I'm here because I want to help. I need to help. Things are too messed up now. I could never go back." Michael clears his throat as if he's about to add more, but doesn't.

"Really?" Jax looks over at me, waiting for a sign. I suspect he's waiting for my head to explode. I know my face is a dark shade of red, but I can't help the emotions that rapidly flow through my body. The only true light in my life, my younger sister, taken, literally right in front of my eyes. No one could lessen the feeling of guilt and anger, even if they tried.

Michael looks down at his clenched hands hanging past his waist. "I know you have no reason to trust me, but I'm here to help." Slowly, Michael releases his fists, revealing a beautiful opalescent stone in his left hand.

"What's this?"

Before he could reply to my question, Kalus springs forward to retrieve the stone.

"This is the culprit! I had a feeling that this powerful stone is the reason for the absence of Alexa's powers." Kalus bellows, "Where did you find this?"

Slowly, Michael answers, "I took it from the queen's room while she was preoccupied with searching for Alexa and Miri. I'm not sure how it works; the only thing I know is that whoever has this in their possession seems to wield Alexa's powers. This is my peace offering. I can help you get Miri back if you can help me get my family back."

Jax quickly shot up and spat back, "Why do you think we would help you when you have been deceiving Alexa since day one?"

Before Michael can answer, I respond, "We will help you, Michael. But from here on out, you need to be nothing but honest and forthcoming with whatever we ask of you. If I find you're not, then there will be consequences." My voice trembles with fury, something I've never experienced before. I scare myself with thoughts of what I would do to the person that took Miri. My threatening stance takes the room by surprise. I feel all eyes on me.

Michael blinks and a look of shock displays across his face. "Certainly, Alexa, anything to make this right. I know it will be hard for you to believe me, but I hope someday you realize that I had no other option but to lie to you."

"I disagree with that. You could have come to me. I saw you everyday at school and you said nothing. This could have been avoided!" My eyes begin to fill, and before anyone can attempt to comfort me, I dash out of the room.

Nothing angers me more than feeling like I'm being lied to or taken advantage of. I've been living my first seventeen years as someone I'm not and I refuse to continue living with blinders on.

The air whips my hair around as I step outside Kasper's house. I need to find Miri and I need to gain back my powers so I can punish whoever took her. Makin's face flashes before me. Then my mind drifts to my mother's face...would she hurt her? Could she possibly be so wretched as everyone says she is?

"Wait up, Alexa!" I hear Kalus coming after me. Can't he take a hint? I want to be alone. Let me guess. He's going to try and be the hero to save Miri and be father of the year...

"I want to be alone," I rudely insist.

"We need to talk, and waiting won't help anyone now. Not with Miri's kidnapping and the fact that we will be facing the queen soon. This can't be put off any longer. I tried to give you space. I tried to leave you alone, but I can't. You're my daughter and the very reason why I live everyday."

I knew Kalus would play the doting father card.

"Listen, Kalus, I know there are probably reasons why you left me on Earth with Elena, but right now isn't the time to explain yourself or make amends. We need to focus on Miri and bringing her back here or wherever." I haven't even thought about where it is we'll reside, but I'm not going to hide from my mother. She's already taken too much from me.

Kalus lets out an exaggerated breath and adds, "You sound just like her."

"Why do you say that? You don't even know me!" How dare he pretend to know me or my inherited traits. "You left me, and you weren't planning on coming back. The only reason you're here is because she found me. You would have let me live my whole life thinking you were dead and that Elena was my real mother. What does that say about you?"

Silence fills the space between us. He opens his mouth to respond but nothing comes out. He silently leaves me like I asked. Clearly, I've won. He won't try and talk to me now, I think in triumph.

Moments pass and the painful absence of Miri only grows, leaving me a ball of nerves.

"Alexa, wait up!" Jax bellows.

"Sure." I tap my foot, anticipating a speech on how I need to give my father a chance.

"Where are you going? Would you like some company?" His aquamarine pools swallow me up whole. How could I ever say no to those eyes?

"I just needed to get away from everyone. When I look at Kalus or Michael, I feel such anger, it's hard to decipher who it's directed at or for what reason since there are so many. Am I this mad because my father left me and has now showed up to fix things? Or am I mad because I didn't see through Michael's lies, and now Miri is gone? I can't help but wonder if I'd just stayed with the queen, my mother, then Miri would be with me and safe." Tears trickle down my face and land on my shirt.

"I get it. I'd be angry, too. I think you're dealing with everything the way anyone would. No one expects you to be understanding with everything that's happened." Jax grabs my hand and an instant shot of electricity pulses through me. "I just want to make sure you're okay." His genuine concern warms me for a minute.

"Why does Kalus try and talk to me now when everything is crazy? He just can't show up and expect me to confide in him. Is he trying to be father of the year?"

"I doubt he thinks that, Alexa. He's upset about Miri, too, and he only wants to get her back and keep you both safe. Think about all of this from his point of view. He left you with Elena to protect you from your mother. He didn't want to walk away from you. He had no choice." The words cut through me, leaving me vulnerable. "From what I hear, he was never very far from you. He's been on Earth following you for a number of years, but he had to keep his distance."

I roll my eyes in response, too exhausted to comment.

The image of my father as Mr. Riley pops into my head. He has been at the high school teaching for the past few years. I did see him daily.

"That doesn't change the fact that he could have told me the truth. At any point, he could have approached me and told me who he was," I quickly counter, leaving Jax speechless.

Silently, we walk into the dense forest, escaping the others as well as our conflicting conversation. A mix of floral scents welcome our entrance. Playfully, Jax squeezes my hand, reminding me that he's still here for me.

"We'll get Miri back, I promise," Jax quietly states.

I want to believe him, but it seems such a huge impossibility. I stare up at the sky and wonder...will I ever see my little sister again?

About the Author

Rebecca Clark is a mother, wife, and science teacher. When she can steal away some quiet time, you will find her reading or following her passion—writing. She enjoys writing young adult fantasy and paranormal romance. When she is not taking care of the family, working, reading, or writing, she enjoys traveling and being with her family and friends. This is the first book in the Stellar Series, and the second book—Disorder—will be out Summer 2016.

Connect with Rebecca Clark

I really appreciate you reading my book! Here are my social media sites:

Follow me on
Twitter: Rebecca_author
Facebook: http://www.facebook.com/thestellarseries
Favorite my Blog: http://rebeccaclarkauthor.com

www.ingramcontent.com/pod-product-compliance
Lightning Source LLC
Chambersburg PA
CBHW020619150626
46552CB00026B/1942